"All right, Detective. I'm willing to listen."

She licked her suddenly dry lips and watched his eyes follow the movement of her tongue, making her skin flush as if it had been caressed.

"I think…I think we can agree that we both want what's best for our son…."

Our son. His words had the effect of a cold bucket of water, making her shiver. "Our son," she whispered aloud with a sad shake of her head. "That will take some getting used to. Tommy has always been *my* son. Just mine."

Their son.

Patrick Sullivan made her want things she knew she could never have.

Be careful what you wish for….

Dear Reader,

August is jam-packed with exciting promotions and top-notch authors in Silhouette Romance! Leading off the month is RITA Award-winning author Marie Ferrarella with *Suddenly...Marriage!,* a lighthearted VIRGIN BRIDES story set in sultry New Orleans. A man and woman, both determined to remain single, exchange vows in a mock ceremony during Mardi Gras, only to learn their bogus marriage is for real....

With over five million books in print, Valerie Parv returns to the Romance lineup with *Baby Wishes and Bachelor Kisses.* In this delightful BUNDLES OF JOY tale, a confirmed bachelor winds up sole guardian of his orphaned niece and must rely on the baby-charming heroine for daddy lessons—*and* lessons in love. Stella Bagwell continues her wildly successful TWINS ON THE DOORSTEP series with *The Ranger and the Widow Woman.* When a Texas Ranger discovers a stranded mother and son, he welcomes them into his home. But the pretty widow harbors secrets this lawman-in-love needs to uncover.

Carla Cassidy kicks off our second MEN! promotion with *Will You Give My Mommy a Baby?* A 911 call from a five-year-old boy lands a single mom and a true-blue, red-blooded hero in a sticky situation that quickly sets off sparks. *USA Today* bestselling author Sharon De Vita concludes her LULLABIES AND LOVE miniseries with *Baby and the Officer.* A crazy-about-kids cop discovers he's a dad, but when he goes head-to-head with his son's beautiful adoptive mother, he realizes he's fallen head over heels. And Martha Shields rounds out the month with *And Cowboy Makes Three,* the second title in her COWBOYS TO THE RESCUE series. A woman who wants a baby and a cowboy who needs an heir agree to marry but discover the honeymoon is just the beginning....

Don't miss these exciting stories by Romance's unforgettable storytellers!

Enjoy,

Joan Marlow Golan

Joan Marlow Golan
Senior Editor Silhouette Books

Please address questions and book requests to:
Silhouette Reader Service
U.S.: 3010 Walden Ave., P.O. Box 1325, Buffalo, NY 14269
Canadian: P.O. Box 609, Fort Erie, Ont. L2A 5X3

BABY AND THE OFFICER

Sharon De Vita

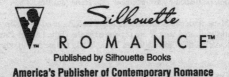

Silhouette

R O M A N C E™

Published by Silhouette Books

America's Publisher of Contemporary Romance

This book is dedicated to the newest published author in
the family: my youngest child and only son,
Anthony Joseph De Vita.
Joey, in less than twelve months, like your sisters before
you, you'll leave home for college. Before you go, I want
you to know how proud I am of the child you were and
the man you've become. I love you.
And don't forget ET's motto: Call home!
Love, Mom

SILHOUETTE BOOKS

ISBN 0-373-19316-5

BABY AND THE OFFICER

Copyright © 1998 by Sharon De Vita

Books by Sharon De Vita

Silhouette Romance

Heavenly Match #475
Lady and the Legend #498
Kane and Mabel #545
Baby Makes Three #573
Sherlock's Home #593
Italian Knights #610
Sweet Adeline #693
†*On Baby Patrol* #1276
†*Baby with a Badge* #1298
†*Baby and the Officer* #1316

Silhouette Special Edition

Child of Midnight #1013
*The Lone Ranger #1078
**The Lady and the Sheriff* #1103
**All It Takes Is Family* #1126

**Silver Creek County*
†*Lullabies and Love*

SHARON DE VITA

is an award-winning author of numerous works of fiction and nonfiction. Her first novel won a national writing competition for Best Unpublished Romance Novel of 1985. This award-winning book, *Heavenly Match*, was subsequently published by Silhouette in 1986.

A frequent guest speaker and lecturer at conferences and seminars across the country, Sharon is currently an Adjunct Professor of Literature and Communications at a private college in the Midwest. With over one million copies of her novels in print, Sharon's professional credentials have earned her a place in *Who's Who in American Authors, Editors and Poets* as well as the *International Who's Who of Authors*. In 1987, Sharon was the proud recipient of *Romantic Times* Lifetime Achievement Award for Excellence in Writing.

She currently makes her home in a small suburb of Chicago, with her two college-age daughters and her teenage son.

Dear Reader,

I'm thrilled to bring you *Baby and the Officer,* the third and last book in my LULLABIES AND LOVE miniseries about the three fabulous Sullivan brothers. *Baby and the Officer* is Patrick's story, and is very, very dear to my heart. As the youngest, Patrick doesn't have the fearlessness of his older brother Danny, nor does he have the worrisome nature of his eldest brother, Michael. Patrick is...the quiet one, the one who hasn't expressed an emotion since the day his beloved father died.

But Patrick's emotions come roaring back to life when he learns that he has a child, a son he never knew about, who was put up for adoption. Devastated, because like all the Sullivans, family means everything to Patrick, he does the one thing—the *only* thing—he can do: he sets out to find and claim his child.

Unfortunately, Sabrina McGee, little Tommy's adoptive mother, has other ideas. Widowed over a year, she doesn't welcome Patrick in her life or her son's. Brie McGee is fighting her own emotional battles, and vows to fight to her death to protect and keep her little boy.

These two wounded people vow to do what is best for the child, but whose best? Come share the love, the laughter and heart-wrenching emotion as these two wonderful people open their hearts and their lives to each other...and an unforgettable love.

Sharon De Vita

Author Note

At the time this book was being written, the adoption laws described in the book were legal in the state of Illinois, where this story takes place. But since these laws vary, please check with your own attorney regarding the adoption laws in your state.

Prologue

Dingle Peninsula
County Kerry, Ireland

He was about to lose the only woman he'd ever loved.

Desolate, he stood atop the jagged cliffs overlooking the foaming waters of Coumeenoole Strand. Night had come quickly, like an impatient lover's arms the darkness had enveloped the barren countryside in a quick, fervent caress. The foaming whitecapped sea rolled slowly toward shore. The soft slapping sound echoed through the darkness, playing a soft, haunting melody that matched his mood.

She would never be his.

He shook his head, unable to believe such blasphemy. But t'was to be. Today at the Puck Fair her clan had pledged her to another.

In front of his shocked eyes, he'd watched as the "wedding matcher" had taken her hand and given it to another, sealing her fate, and dooming his.

It had broken his heart.

Bitter, he'd thought of all the plans they'd made. Since they were wee ones they'd known they were destined for each other. She was his other half; his soul.

He'd known it the moment he'd laid eyes on her. With her fiery red hair, dancing green eyes and lips that could make the angels sing, one glance at her and he'd lost his tender heart forever.

He knew he would never—could never love another.

He thought of all the plans they'd made in the quiet of night when they'd snuck out to these jagged cliffs and held each other tightly, whispering of their love, their future, their sons. He thought now of the life they'd craved, the dreams they'd spun, the plans they'd made. For the future; their future.

He thought of the cradle he'd carved with such care. Intricate and beautiful, it was to be a wedding gift for his love, for the strong, strapping sons she would bless him with. Sons who would carry his name and one day have sons of their own, sons who would one day fulfill their own destiny, find their own true love.

And one day have sons of their own.

The cradle was to have been a thread from one generation to another, to be given when each had found their own true love. The cradle was to serve as a remembrance of those who had come before them, of the enormous love they'd been a part of and shared, of the memories and traditions that had been carried on by the Sullivan Clan for centuries.

Alas, it was to have been his and Molly's legacy; a precious keepsake for future generations of the clan so they would always know of their endless, enduring love.

Aye, now he knew it was for naught.

Impotently his fists clenched and he took a deep breath,

letting it out slowly. Now, he wanted to toss the cradle into the foaming sea, to watch the smooth, fine wood crash and splinter against the rocks, the way his heart had been splintered.

She was never to be his.

No!

He shook his head. He couldn't bear the thought.

A cold, bitter drizzle began to fall, hiding his tears.

His heart ached for he knew there would never be another love. Not for him.

Only Molly.

Watching the foaming sea, his chin lifted; pride and anger surged through him.

He was a Sullivan, one of six brothers. They were a proud, strong clan and did not take defeat lightly. They'd been taught to fight for what was rightfully theirs. To do any less would bring shame to their name and their clan. Something no Sullivan would ever allow.

He would not sit by and let his only love slip away. Nay, he couldn't, not and live with himself. There'd be no reason for living if she wasn't his.

Molly belonged to him as surely as if they'd been tethered together at birth.

He knew it and so did she.

Defeat was not a word he could live with, nay, not and live with himself. Pride, love and his aching heart refused to accept what destiny had decried.

He could not allow her to marry another no matter what her clan dictated.

Determined now, he turned his face to the sea, letting the soft mist and the brisk wind bathe his face.

He'd been gifted with an equal amount of temper and reason. He knew he'd need both now, to think, to plan. His future—their future—depended on it, and so did the future of the Sullivan clan.

He thought of the cradle again, and determination filled him, strengthening his resolve and curling his fists.

He still had time, a chance perhaps. Molly's match was set for morn'. He still had a few hours left, and maybe just maybe...

Smiling now, he turned from the foaming sea. He knew now what he must do.

His life, their life and the destiny of the clan depended on it.

Chapter One

It was a simple, single letter that shattered Detective Patrick Sullivan's life.

"The postman's here to see you, Patrick." Sean Patrick Sullivan, Patrick's grandfather, and the eighty-six-year-old patriarch of the Sullivan family whom everyone affectionately called Da, wiped his hands on his ever-present white apron and nodded toward the mailman who was poking his head through the swinging doorway of the kitchen of Sullivan's Pub.

"Probably another love letter from one of your lovely lasses," Da said with a chuckle. His blue eyes, so like his youngest grandson's, twinkled mischievously as he waved the postman into the room, then turned his attention back to the stew he had simmering for the dinner rush.

"You Patrick Sullivan?" The mailman stepped into the room, regarding him carefully.

"I am." Stuffing the last of his sandwich into his mouth, Patrick wiped his hands on a napkin, then signed for the letter with a frown, wondering what could be so important that a law firm had to send him a special delivery letter.

For a moment, he stared at the envelope. For some reason, he felt a dark sense of foreboding.

He tore open the envelope, and slowly began to read. The letter was from an attorney for a woman he used to date.

Barbara Keats. He and Barbara had dated for several months a few years ago. For a while he'd thought it might become something more than just a casual relationship, until one day Barbara just up and disappeared without warning, without a word. For weeks he'd called her repeatedly, but there was never any answer, and then, her number had been disconnected.

Concerned, he'd gone to her apartment, only to find it stripped and bare. He went to her place of employment, only to be told quite coldly that she'd been transferred to another office in Chicago and, no, they would not be willing to part with her new address.

Frustrated, he'd tried for several more weeks to charm, cajole and coddle the information from her employer, and then finally he'd given up, realizing for some odd reason that Barbara didn't want to be found, at least not by him. His ego had been a bit bruised, but he was a Sullivan and had plenty of ego to go around.

And so he'd let it be and forgotten about her.

Until this cool afternoon in September when a special delivery letter had arrived from her attorney.

Tossing the envelope into the trash, Patrick continued to read quickly, curiosity getting the better of him.

For a moment, the words didn't register and he stared blankly at the page, totally confused. The din of the kitchen, the scent of the stew simmering, the fans blowing, the dishwasher humming faded into oblivion as he struggled to understand, realizing his mind, like the moment, seemed somehow to have been frozen in time. Shaking his head a bit, he began reading again, letting the words slowly seep in.

A baby.

A child.

Barbara had had a child.

His child.

The words slammed into him, nearly knocking him senseless. He sank back down in his chair, his mind whirling. This couldn't be. Unconsciously his fingers tightened on the page, wrinkling the edges. Barbara was dead, killed in an freak car accident in the south of France, nearly three months ago. She had instructed her attorney to notify him of the child's birth only upon her death.

Hands shaking, Patrick read the letter again, certain he'd been mistaken. But there it was in black and white. There was also a handwritten note on lovely lavender stationery from Barbara confirming the information.

The explanation he'd longed for three years ago was now unfolding in front of him. Barbara had discovered she was expecting within days of being offered a promotion and transfer. It was a promotion she'd been working toward for two long years. Torn, she knew that if she'd told him about the child, he'd insist they marry. Marriage had never been in her plans, nor had a child, but she knew he would never be able to understand that. And so she'd gratefully accepted the promotion and the transfer, carried her pregnancy to term and given the child up for adoption *without ever telling him*.

Raising a hand to his suddenly throbbing head, Patrick's mind clouded and his eyes swam.

He had a child.

Dear God.

It wasn't possible.

A child he had never known about until this moment.

Emotions warred, then swamped him. Rage, frustration and futility overwhelmed him.

How could she have done this to him?

How could she have kept this knowledge from him?

He leaned back against the chair, letting his eyes close and a long heartfelt sigh escape. How could she have made a decision like that, a decision that would forever alter so many lives without ever letting him know?

The injustice of the situation, of her decision, slammed into him, and he felt the bite of her cruelty all the way to his soul.

Knowing him, how could Barbara have done such a thing?

She'd met his family—his mother, Maeve; his grandfather, Da; met his older brothers, Michael and Danny, as well. She'd always known how important, how necessary, family was to him—to all of them.

The Sullivans were a loud, proud, boisterous group, but as tight as twine and as close-knit as the long-ago clans that had inherited and inhabited their homeland.

Family came first and foremost—always—with the Sullivans. And children—well, children were a blessing, a joy to be cherished, celebrated, loved.

Not given away like a misbehaved puppy.

The mere thought ripped at his insides and he felt a pain unlike anything he'd ever known grip his heart.

She'd given away his child.

His child!

Patrick's eyes blurred. The cruelty of her actions were beyond imagination.

He was a man raised with the tradition of family. Like all of the late Jock Sullivan's boys, he'd learned at an early age what was expected of him. Duty, family and responsibility to yourself, your family and community weren't just words, but a way of life.

For as long as he could remember, he knew what had been expected of him—of all of them. Being a Sullivan meant something. With his name came pride, heritage and tradition.

His family had always been the backbone of his life. The stability and security from which everything else emanated. Any storm, any problem could be weathered, for it was never weathered alone. His family was always there— would always be there. It brought a comfort to his life that he rarely thought of.

Until now.

He'd always held the dream of one day passing on his name and his family's heritage and traditions to his own child; of carrying on the Sullivan name in the same way so many had done before him.

But he'd been robbed of the opportunity by the careless act of a selfish woman.

His child would never know the security or the heritage of being a Sullivan. His child would never know what it was like to grow up with the history and traditions that had marked all of their lives with indelible ink that would carry on for generations to come.

The truth lay like an anvil on his chest, making breathing difficult. Patrick forced himself to be calm, to continue reading, anxious and hoping for some small bit of information, some clue that would tell him of his child.

It was a boy—a son—born just over two years ago. The knowledge made his heart soar, leap, then plummet. Barbara had arranged for a private adoption through her Chicago attorney.

Sabrina and Dennis McGee.

McGee.

Patrick blinked. They were Irish. It was a small fact that wedged in his memory as the gravity of the situation seeped in.

Barbara was dead.

His natural human instincts were to grieve for the passing of a woman he had known, a woman who had borne his child, but he couldn't. Not now. Not yet. His emotions were too raw.

Rereading the letter quickly, his strong fingers threatened to crush the lovely lavender paper.

"Patrick, son, is there a problem?" Da stood next to him, his large, beefy hand calm and steady on his shoulder. There was a bit of worry in his eyes, dimming the twinkle.

Blinking away tears, Patrick glanced up at the grandfather who had been so much a part of his life. Patrick had lost his own father in the line of duty when he'd been eight years old. He knew what it was like to grow up without the benefit of the loving hand of a father.

But he'd had Da.

Da had always been there for him, for all of them. Da was and always had been the backbone of the Sullivan family. The calm, steady anchor through all of life's storms.

Still, it hadn't entirely eased the pain of losing his father. Nothing ever could. The loss of a father marked and shaped a boy's life as nothing else. It left a gaping hole in the heart that nothing—absolutely nothing could ever fill.

He'd never let his son experience such pain.

Abruptly, he stood with such force he knocked his chair over backward.

"Patrick?"

Da stared at the young man in surprise. Of all his grandsons, Patrick was the one he worried about most. Aye, not because he was the youngest, although there was worry enough in that. Nay, he worried most about Patrick because he was the quiet one, the somber one. The one who held everything inside.

As the oldest, Mikey was calm and steady as an anchor. Danny, as the middle child, had always been a rebel. But then again, Da realized with a bit of pride, Danny had always been the most like him. Fearless and unflappable, Danny had, at times, more grit than common sense, but a finer man you'd never find.

But it was Patrick, aye, quiet, solemn Patrick, who'd caused him the most worry, perhaps because he'd never given him a moment *of* worry.

Since his father's death, Patrick had seemed to curl up somewhere deep inside himself. While his older brothers could be hellions—and were at times—Patrick was always calm, reasonable...quiet.

Da had worried that Patrick would explode from the emotions he'd kept so bottled up. Not since the day of his father's death had he seen Patrick shed a tear or express any emotion. It worried him, aye, more than he'd ever let on. He'd loved his grandsons equally, just as he'd loved all his children equally, but Patrick had always held a soft spot in his heart.

"Patrick, son, what's troubling you?"

Patrick shook his dark head. He couldn't speak. There were too many thoughts, too many emotions, swirling around inside. He merely handed his grandfather the lawyer's letter, then turned and pushed through the swinging door.

"Patrick?" Da went after him, pausing at the door, his aged face creased with worry. "Where is it that you're going in such a fine hurry?"

Patrick didn't answer. He couldn't. His throat was clogged with pain and fear.

He knew where he was going. The only place he could go.

To find and claim the son who had so cruelly been stolen from him.

"Brie, that man's outside again, staring through the glass as if to burn a hole through it with his eyes." Standing behind the counter of Wishes and Whims, Fiona McGee scowled at the man over her reading spectacles. "He's a handsome one, I'll give you that, even if he is as big as a sequoia, but a bit suspicious, don't you think?" She sniffed, keeping an eagle eye on the man. "Been here two days in a row, doing nothing but…looking as if he expected to find the wisdom of the ages printed on those panes."

Sabrina McGee, known as Brie to her family and friends, laughed softly as she adjusted the hem on a display set of curtains emblazoned with toy trains. The entire display was a perfect replica of a gaily decorated bedroom, destined to fulfill any little boy's dreams and fuel his imagination.

Completely coordinated in primary colors deliberately designed to catch the eye, Brie had lovingly picked out and put together every single item in every display bedroom in the store. Next to her son, the design store was her pride and joy.

Every child's wish, every child's whim for a wonderful room of their own, filled with imagination and dreams, could be found at Wishes and Whims. She prided herself on it.

Brie cocked a brow at her late husband's grandmother. At seventy-six, Fiona McGee had the energy and the spirit of a woman half her age. Not to mention the temper.

"And since when are you complaining about a handsome man peering in at you?" Brie asked with a laugh, lifting the hem of the curtain to check the stitching. Satisfied, she let it drop, then wandered to another display.

"Only when I think he's a bit daft," Fiona snapped back, smoothing a hand over her cap of snow-white hair. "And two days of staring marks a man as daft in my book." Her arthritic hands fluttered nervously. "Especially if he has the handsome looks of the devil. Look busy, Brie," the older woman said abruptly. "I think he's finally coming in."

Glancing at the door where the overhead bell tinkled, signaling a customer, Brie left the display to greet their customer, curiosity getting the best of her.

She, too, had noticed the man standing outside, just... watching for the past couple of days. It was nothing out of the ordinary. Their displays were designed to catch attention, but usually it was a five- or six-year-old peering in the window, eyes bright, their noses pressed against the panes.

"May I help you?" Giving him her brightest smile, Brie glanced up and felt something jolt her heart, nearly stopping it. He was, she instantly decided, far too handsome to be walking about freely, not without giving some poor lass heart fits.

His hair was as black as a raven's wing. His features were harsh and yet somehow beautiful. Bleak, but beautiful in their own way.

His eyes were a shade of blue she'd not seen since she'd left Ireland. They reminded her of the bountiful sky on a cloudless morn. But there was something in those eyes, a hint of anger, of suspicion. It instantly set her nerves on edge, perhaps because for the first time since her husband's death nearly a year ago, she'd found herself responding to a man on a purely physical level. And it frightened and surprised her, for she was certain the time for such female frivolities had passed.

"May I help you?" she repeated, wishing her voice sounded stronger, steadier. Nervous now, she linked her slender hands together, letting them come to rest in front of her so that he wouldn't see the nerves that made her fingers tremble. An odd feeling suffused her. Not discomfort really, but something else, something she couldn't identify at the moment.

There was something about the man, something that seemed entirely too familiar, as if she had known him before. Immediately she dismissed the thought, knowing it was impossible, even silly. She'd never laid eyes on him in her life. If she had, she certainly would have remembered. He had the kind of face a woman wasn't likely to forget.

Patrick could only stare, his gaze riveted on the small, slender woman standing before him. The moment his eyes connected with hers, it seemed as if he'd lost his ability to speak. She was in a word…incredible.

Rich, vibrant hair the color of fire cascaded down her back in a tightly coiled, intricate braid that nearly reached her slender waist. Her eyes were a clear, deep blue, clear and bright as the most expensive sapphires. Her skin was the color of alabaster, pale, yet delicate with only a hint of coloring touching her high, chiseled cheeks. Her lips were lush and full, touched with a bit of wickedly shiny gloss, making him wonder what it would be like to feel those lips on his.

Dressed in black leggings that hugged her slender legs, and an oversize black sweater belted at her waist, the high turtleneck collar caressed the gentle curve of her chin, making her seem even paler and more fragile.

Still staring at him, and waiting, Brie frowned a bit, laying a hand on his arm in concern.

"May I help you?" she asked again, a bit louder in case

the man was not only daft, as dear Fiona had predicted, but a wee bit deaf, as well.

Patrick shook his head, trying to shake off the spell he was certain she'd ensnared him in the moment he'd stepped into her store.

The heat of her hand burned through the long sleeves of his shirt. He felt as if he'd taken a sucker punch to the gut. It had been a long time—years—since the mere sight of a woman had knocked him off his axis. He was far too stable, too centered, to be knocked for a loop by a woman. Or he had been until he'd stepped into this magical store and come face-to-face with her.

Struggling to gain some perspective, Patrick tried to infuse his voice, his stance with professionalism. "Are you Sabrina McGee?"

His tone was hard. As if he'd suddenly discovered something entirely unpleasant about her. Why it annoyed her, she wasn't certain.

Piqued, one dark brow rose in question as she let her hand drop from his arm. The man had instantly put her on guard.

"And who is it that's asking?"

There was no mistaking the hint of temper in her voice and Patrick's nerves finally relented enough to allow him to smile. Her accent was unmistakable. It held the same, soft lilting tones he'd been hearing all his life from Da. Something warm and entirely too familiar wrapped around Patrick's guarded heart.

"You're Irish." It wasn't a question, but a statement, as if confirming some wonderful secret only he was privy to. Relief flooded through him and if pressed, he couldn't explain why. His smile widened and he felt his heart finally begin to slide back into a normal rhythm as his tense muscles relaxed.

"Aye," she said with a nod of her head and a bit of a smile she couldn't contain. His voice had changed. It was gentler now, yet still held that deep, rough masculinity that had sent a deep, dark shiver skimming up her spine. "Guilty as charged."

"Where are you from?" He couldn't stop staring at her. He fought the impulse to reach out and stroke a finger down her cheek, to see if that skin was as silky and soft as it looked.

Her chin angled and her eyes flashed. The handsome stranger with the harsh face and the bleak eyes was excellent at asking questions, but not so efficient at answering them.

"And why is it you want to know?" she asked, tilting her chin a bit to meet his gaze even though it made her feel as if a flock of sparrows had taken flight in her tummy.

Patrick debated for only a moment, before reaching in his back pocket for his wallet. He flipped it open and held it up so she could see the gold badge.

It had taken him nearly a week to find her, and then another two days to get up the courage to come inside. Now that he was here, face-to-face with the woman who *had* his son, he had no idea how to proceed. He'd been going strictly on emotions, not thinking out the consequences of his actions, fueled only by the desperate need to find his son.

He'd learned as much as possible about Sabrina McGee in the past week. He'd learned about her shop, located in a very trendy part of Chicago, near Wrigley Field in an area known as Wrigleyville.

Surrounded by refurbished brownstones and high-paid young executives, the area was teeming with small, exclusive specialty shops that catered to the well-heeled young families who had begun moving back into the now-thriving area that still carried a hint of seediness from its declining years.

He'd learned she'd lost her husband a year ago to cancer. At the time, the knowledge had shocked him, because it meant his son was being raised by a woman alone, without the benefit of a strong male presence.

Not that a woman couldn't raise a child alone. On the contrary, his own mother had been a single parent for most of his life, but Da had always been there with a kind word and a loving, male hand.

His son would not have Da in his life.

At least, not if he let things be. Something he had no intention of doing.

How to proceed, Patrick wondered again, realizing the situation was far more complicated than he'd anticipated. Cautiously, he decided. Just as he had proceeded with anything and everything that had ever truly mattered to him. With caution, and more than a bit of delicacy.

"I'm Patrick Sullivan." He carefully watched her expression, wanting—needing—to see if there was any recognition of his name. There wasn't. "*Detective* Patrick Sullivan."

He had no idea if she'd been told anything of her child's biological father. Or if, like him, she'd been kept in the dark as well. There were so many questions, and unfortunately, at the moment, not nearly enough answers.

Stunned, Brie stared at the badge for a moment, then slowly lifted her gaze to his, totally confused.

"*Garda?*" She shook her head, then reverted back to English. "You're a police officer?"

She never would have thought him an officer of the law. He was dressed more like one of the busy executives who frequented her shop on his day off. He wore slender, crisply pressed jeans that only emphasized the long length of his legs. His shirt, in a fine shade of blue that mirrored his eyes, was just as finely pressed, with the collar turned up a bit. His ebony jacket was almost as dark as his hair, and looked to be some sort of pigskin. Leather. That was what it was, she decided.

So, it was a police officer he was, she thought with a hint of a frown. He certainly didn't resemble the middle-age neighborhood police officer who rode his motorbike around dressed in a wrinkled uniform, and scuffed black boots.

And why had he been just longingly staring into the windows for two blessed days like a lovesick bovine? she wondered, her confusion growing.

"I guess it's my turn to confess." He grinned the famous Sullivan grin, and a dimple flashed. "I am indeed a police officer."

Brie laughed softly, shaking her head in obvious relief. His smile had changed his entire face, totally disarming her.

Sullivan, she thought with a small nod. Irish. *Black* Irish, she mentally corrected. Kinship should have brought approval; she found it only alarmed her. In her experience, limited as it was, she'd found that Irish men with looks like his had a tendency to be all charm and no substance. Sort of like one of those delightfully sinful pastries the baker down the street specialized in. Beautiful and sinfully tempting on the outside, what with their chocolate swirls and rich whipped cream, but the inside, ah, the inside was little more than flimsy layers of puffed air.

Policeman or not, considering his bizarre behavior she still wondered if he might be a bit daft. The thought made her laugh again.

The sound of her soft laughter skittered along Patrick's nerve endings, making him feel alive for the first time in a long time. That sound made him want—need—desire, and he knew it was dangerous. Far too dangerous, especially with a woman, particularly *this* woman. He had to keep a tight rein on his emotions. He had far too much at stake.

"A policeman it is? Well, then, why didn't you just say so, Detective?" Smiling, Brie held out her hand. He stared at it for a moment. "I am indeed Sabrina McGee, and this," she said with a wave of her hand, "is my store."

Patrick took her hand, letting the texture of her skin embrace his. Her hand was soft, warm and incredibly feminine. He had a strong desire to lift her hand to his lips, but resisted. Instead, he closed his hand over hers for a moment, allowing the rush of purely physical feelings to rock him for a moment.

He caught a hint of her feminine scent, probably from some cream she'd lathered on her hands. It was sweet and sensual and he couldn't help but wonder if she smelled like that all over.

His gaze met hers and he found himself instantly intrigued by the quick flash of confusion in the depths of her clear blue eyes. She couldn't hide anything. Not her thoughts, not her emotions. Her eyes reflected them all.

So he'd touched her as well, he realized. It should have stunned him, but it merely settled and pleased him, and he didn't pause to wonder why. As Da had always told them, some things in life were not meant to be explained, for there was no explanation that would suffice.

Alarmed at her reaction to his touch, Brie slid her hand from his, resisting the urge to swipe it down the length of cloth that covered her legs to diffuse some of the tingle of heat. She would not show her nervousness. It was nothing but foolishness, plain and simple. She was a grown woman with a child, not a simpering adolescent with too many hormones and too little common sense to be knocked off base by a handsome face and a charming smile.

"So, you're a police officer, you say?" Fiona had crept up toward the front of the shop, and now stood peering at them from behind the protection of a white canopy bed fringed in delicate pink and white lace.

Fiona's words seemed to break the spell and Brie turned with a laugh, grateful for the diversion.

"Detective Sullivan, this is Fiona McGee. My grandmother-in-law and partner." It was an awkward statement and entirely inadequate for a woman who had meant so much to her for so long.

"I'm pleased to meet you," Patrick said, extending his hand toward the older woman. For an instant, she looked at it suspiciously, as if it contained some secret poison potion, but then she smiled, coming around the corner of the display to take Patrick's hand, shaking it firmly.

"You're a big one, you are," she commented, tilting her head back to look at him. All of him.

Patrick laughed. "You should see my brothers."

"You have brothers, do you?" Fiona was still holding on to his hand. There was something calm and stable about this man, nothing she could put her finger on, but something she could nevertheless identify. Seventy-six years of living had given her some wisdom, even about men.

"Two." Patrick retrieved his hand and slipped it in his pocket, realizing he was nervous. "Michael is the oldest and about two inches taller than me."

"Taller?" Fiona's eyes widened. "Two inches, you say?" She shook her head in disbelief. "And the other brother?" she asked with a frown.

"Danny?" Patrick laughed. "He's only about an inch taller." His gaze shifted to Brie, and he was pleased to find her staring at him intently. "I'm the runt of the family."

"Runt?" Fiona frowned, obviously not understanding, turning to Brie for a translation.

Brie laid a gentle hand on her arm. "It means the last born and the smallest, I think?" She glanced at Patrick for confirmation and he nodded, pleasing her.

"So, Detective." Turning back to him, Brie slipped her hands in her pockets. "I'm very glad to finally meet you."

"You are?" Confused, Patrick watched her, wondering what was going on.

"Why, yes," Brie confirmed, rocking back on her heels with a relieved smile. "I've been expecting you."

Chapter Two

Chapter Two

He lifted a dark brow. "Expecting me?"

Tilting her head back, Brie grinned up at him as if she was enjoying herself immensely. She rather liked the look of surprise on his face. It softened the harsh lines of his features and made him look far more appealing. Not quite so intimidating.

Quickly she banished the thought, ashamed. She was widowed just over a year; she had no business ogling other men, no matter how fine-looking they were. It was disloyal to her late husband's memory, not to mention her own resolve about men. Her marriage had taught her to be extremely cautious and careful about men, especially handsome, Irish men. A poor choice could leave scars and cobwebs on a woman's heart. It had hers.

"You look…surprised, Detective," she said with some curiosity.

"I confess I am." *Surprised* wasn't quite the word he was thinking of, but it would do. For now.

And did she have to keep smiling up at him like that?

he wondered in sudden annoyance. It made him feel as if he was looking into the face of a beautiful angel.

Over the years he'd met, been attracted to and even been enchanted by any number of women, but none had ever had the immediate impact this woman had had on him. It not only annoyed him, it scared the hell out of him.

This was the one woman in the world he couldn't afford to be softheaded or softhearted around, never mind attracted to. He had far too much at stake to consider letting wayward testosterone overrule his heart or his intellect.

For his son's sake, he had to keep his wits about him. At least until he was certain exactly what she was up to. She hadn't appeared to recognize his name, so why on earth had she been expecting him?

Did she know who he really was?

More important, did she know *why* he was here?

Had she, too, perhaps gotten a deathbed confession letter from Barbara?

He wasn't certain. Not liking the shaky ground he was standing on, Patrick studied her face, and decided to tread very, very carefully until he had some idea what was going on and exactly how much she knew about him and the current situation.

After years as a cop, he'd grown adept at judging the subtleties of human nature. It wasn't hard to figure out when someone was lying to him, or being less than honest. He should be able to tell rather quickly what she was about; all he needed was to spend a little time with her. Just enough to talk to her, to draw her out. The more knowledge he had, the better prepared he would be, and the easier it would be to draw up a plan of action.

Studying her now, he looked into her upturned face, complete with its smattering of freckles. He expected to find some hint of deceit, deception; instead, he found only mild curiosity.

As much as he liked looking at her, he shifted his glance and noticed Fiona had disappeared.

"I *did* call you," Brie finally pointed out.

His head jerked back and his gaze once again met hers. A scowl drew his brows together. "You what?"

Unfailingly even tempered, Brie sighed patiently. "I called you, Detective," she repeated slowly so he'd be certain to understand. "Several days ago. Three to be exact."

Totally confused, Patrick slipped his hands in his jacket. "Called me, did you?" he asked with a skeptical lift of his brow.

Still nervous by the way he was gaping at her, Brie reached out and straightened the corner of a baby blue-and-white gingham comforter on a delicate white scrolled youth bed that didn't need to be straightened.

"Yes, Detective. I believe I just stated that." If all of the police were as thickheaded as this one, it was no wonder there was so much crime in the city.

Cocking his head, Patrick studied her. "And exactly what did you call me about?"

Blowing out a breath, Brie pushed a tumble of loose tendrils off her forehead, praying for patience. "I called about my alarm, Detective." She peered up into his face. "Three days ago," she repeated for the poor man's sake. "Remember?"

Frustrated, Patrick shook his head. "Yes, I got the three days ago part, it's the alarm part that I'm not getting." Dawning recognition made him realize that perhaps he'd been presented with a golden opportunity. He decided to follow her lead. "You think I'm here because of an alarm?"

"Certainly." It was her turn to look confused. "Why

else would the police be here?'' she asked with a frown. She studied him for a moment. "You *are* here about my alarm, aren't you?'' A flash of some unbidden sense of fear washed over her and for some reason her heart began to pound. She needed to explain, if only for her own sense of assurance.

"You see, my insurance fellow told me that if I put an alarm into the store, it would set my rates lower. I had the thing installed and hooked up to the police station, except now the blasted thing keeps going off. Which is why I called you, or rather the station.''

"I see.'' Patrick glanced around, for the first time taking a good look at his surroundings. Though the shop was rather limited in space, it was packed to the rafters with appealing bedroom displays composed of bright colors, fascinating lights and eye-appealing accents. It was designed to catch the imagination and the eye of any child under the age of twelve, or over the age of thirty.

His gaze was drawn to a bedroom done in a sports motif of black, white and red in honor of Chicago's beloved Bulls basketball team. Numerous trinkets and sports paraphernalia adorned and complemented the spread, drapes and sheets. Matching wallpaper and a small basketball hoop adorned the walls. It was the kind of bedroom any little boy would love; a place that would allow him to dream of jump shots and rebounds.

Her store was a visual feast for the eyes and the imagination. Impressed, he turned back to her. "Did you do all this yourself?''

Pleased, she smiled. "Yes. Fiona and I started the business two years ago, and together we've managed to make quite a success out of it.''

She didn't explain the frustrations she'd encountered or the worry about finances and vendors they'd experienced during their first year in business, not to mention fighting her husband every step of the way. He'd resented the store, he'd resented the baby, he'd resented anything that caused her attention to be on anything other than him.

But stubbornness and determination were traits she was blessed with—cursed with, some would say—and she refused to give up on her dreams, in spite of a man who didn't believe in anything as frivolous as a woman's dreams.

Feeling pleased and proud, Brie glanced around. Oh, they'd had problems, to be sure, but she and Fiona had handled them competently. Efficiently, but not without a few dark moments. But now, finally, it looked as if they might actually turn a profit this year.

He nodded. "Yes, I can see that."

"Anyway…" Her voice trailed off. She wanted to get him back to the problem at hand. It was almost three and her son would be up from his nap any moment, then Fiona would take over in the store so she could devote herself to her child. "Detective Sullivan, if you please, I'd like to talk about—"

"Yes, your alarm." He crossed his arms across his chest and leaned against one of the partitions. "So tell me, have they all been false alarms?"

He thought of her shop being victimized, of *her* being victimized and a flash of something strongly resembling protectiveness rose to the surface. His son was living with this woman. If she was in danger, that meant his son might possibly be in danger. The thought immediately raised Patrick's hackles and his gut-level response was to demand the return of his son so he could take him to the safety and security of his own family home.

That was not an option, however, no matter how much it appealed to him. The situation was the most delicate he'd ever encountered. There were too many issues that would have to be dealt with, issues of both morality and legality. He might be her child's biological father, but she was still the child's legal parent and guardian. They both had a claim to the child, or so he'd been told.

It was definitely a dicey situation, and what he absolutely didn't want to do was spook her. She could, if she wanted, simply banish him from his son's life, and be well within her rights and there would be absolutely nothing he could do about it.

He knew. He'd asked.

Before he'd even ventured looking for her, he'd called his cousin Peter, who was an attorney, in order to get the full legal ramifications of the situation.

They weren't particularly bright.

But he wasn't about to let that stop him.

He might be a cop, and it might be his job to uphold the laws, but for the first time in his adult life, Patrick realized that the law didn't take into account very human feelings and emotions, not to mention unusual situations.

How could laws dictate feelings? He was the child's biological father and no law in the world was ever going to change that.

Struggling to understand the man, Brie's brows knit together. "The alarm, yes, well… I had it installed at the suggestion of my insurance agent after we had a break-in here a few months back. But I reported it to your station house and they sent out someone to investigate and do all the other things police matters necessitate. Some of your fellow officers were here for several days, and made detailed notes and reports." Her frown deepened. "I thought for sure you'd have kept a record of it."

Trying to appear casual, he glanced around. "Yeah, well, I haven't actually seen the reports." It wasn't a lie. He hadn't seen the reports—yet. But he would. He wanted to know everything about Sabrina McGee and her shop and her life. "I'm a detective in the gang crimes unit—"

Thoroughly confused and a bit off balance, Brie raised her hand in the air. "Wait a minute, Detective. Could you back up a bit, please? What do you mean you're with the gang crimes unit?"

"It's a special investigative unit, part of the police department that deals specifically with crimes involving organized gangs."

"You think the break-in at my store was done by a gang?" she asked with a bit of trepidation. She'd been in America, and the city of Chicago, long enough to understand about gangs, but she'd never imagine that they'd touch her life or her world.

"Not necessarily," Patrick lied, feeling a hint of guilt at his deception. He hadn't meant to scare her, but judging from how pale her face had gone, he'd done just that. Considering what was at stake, he realized he'd had no choice. "I'm sure there's nothing to be concerned about, but just as a precautionary measure I wanted to come out and ask you a few questions and do a little…digging, maybe keep the store under surveillance for a few days."

He had an urge to touch his nose to see if it had grown. He hadn't told so many lies since he was six years old and gotten suspended from school for punching Eric Whiler out over Mary Mullins, who had been the great love of his young life.

"But I don't understand, Detective." Brie shook her head, sending her braid swaying. "No one mentioned to me that an officer might be keeping the store under surveillance." She was desperately trying not to be frightened. But she was a woman alone, responsible for a small child and an elderly relative. The thought that they might be in any hint of danger was more than a little alarming.

"There was no reason to tell you, Mrs. McGee—"

"Brie, please Detective," she said almost offhandedly. She wanted no reminders of her late marital state.

He gave a quick nod. "Brie it is, then. As I said, this is just a precautionary measure. I'm merely going to be taking a look around." He smiled, hoping to soothe her fears. "You have some big-ticket items in here, as well as lots of expensive sports items and dolls," he added as his gaze traveled the shop again, making a mental note of the value of the items. "It was probably just kids looking to make a quick score, but—"

She shook her head and held up her hand again. "I'm sorry, Detective, but you're going to have to speak English to me. An English I understand." One auburn brow rose. "Big-ticket items? Quick scores?" She shook her head again. "Translation, please?"

Patrick's smile was quick. It was clear that some of the nuances of American slang were lost on her. It was to be expected, he supposed. Even after all these years, American slang still had the ability to befuddle Da, something that still amused everyone in the family.

Charmed in spite of himself, Patrick patiently began to explain. "Big-ticket items are things that can be stolen and then resold at a high price. And I've no doubt the break-in was nothing but neighborhood teens looking to make some fast money selling stolen goods, but since there's been a problem with gang activity in the past in this area, we want to be certain there hasn't been a resurgence." Glancing around, he slipped his hands in his pockets again. "As I said, it's merely a precautionary measure."

"I see," she said, feeling a bit unsettled. "Exactly how long will it take you to know whether this was gang related or not?'' She didn't want to have to consider the real possibility that she or her family might be in jeopardy.

"Probably just a few days," he explained with ease, knowing that would give him more than enough time to find out what he needed to know, and hopefully work out a plan that would give him some direction as to how to proceed. "I'll be hanging around, keeping an eye on things." He studied her face. "I hope that won't be a problem?''

"No, no, of course not." She shifted her gaze, not certain she wanted to acknowledge what she felt every time she looked into those gloriously blue eyes. "I'm more than willing to cooperate with the police department.''

She slipped her hands in the pockets of her oversize sweater, far more nervous than the situation called for. The idea of having the very, very attractive Irish detective hanging around for a few days was very unsettling.

"So I guess this means you're not here to fix my alarm?'' she asked with a rueful smile.

Displaying his large hands, Patrick grinned. "Afraid not. These hands are all thumbs when it comes to anything mechanical, but I'll be more than happy to take a look at it if you like. But I can't promise anything.''

Brie scowled. "That blasted alarm has been more trouble than it's worth. Even though we live upstairs, it's not often we can hear everything that's going on down here, especially during the night.''

"We?'' He tried not to show his anxiety. Tried not to let on the way his heart was pounding.

"Fiona, me and my son. We live together in a large apartment over the store.''

"You have a son?'' he asked carefully, and she nodded. A beautiful smile lit her face.

"Yes, a little boy. He's just over two and quite bright.''

She laughed. "He's also a holy terror at times. The terrible twos, you know."

Unfortunately he didn't know.

"And your husband?" He let the words hang in the air and saw the quick darkening of her eyes. He wasn't certain what the emotion was behind the look, if it was grief, anger or disappointment. All he knew was that the mention of her husband had brought a definite change to her face.

"I'm a widow," she said quietly, clearly uncomfortable discussing this bit of business with him. Abruptly she glanced at her watch, then frowned. "It's almost three, Detective, and my son should be waking from his afternoon nap at any moment, so if you don't mind, could we finish this—" Her voice broke off as a door at the back of the shop flew open and a high-pitched squeal filled the air.

"Ma-ma." A chubby, black-haired toddler scrambled into the store, with Fiona fast on his heels trying to keep up.

Fiona huffed as she tried to catch the scrambling child. "Tommy, my boy, I'm too old to be chasing tornadoes."

Giggling loudly, and obviously delighted with the game of avoid-Grandma-Fiona, the toddler barreled toward his mother, sidestepping his way through the room to avoid a collision with all the displays. Laughing and squealing, he resembled a small, drunken sailor who'd had one too many pints of ale.

"Ma-ma," he squealed again. With a giggle, he threw himself against Brie's legs and held on tight.

"So you're up from your nap then." Smiling tenderly, she reached down and petted his hair as he turned his face up to her. He had something sticky and green smeared all over his mouth and enmeshed in his hair.

"Hot dog?" he asked expectantly, giving her a charming grin and raising his arms to be lifted.

Brie laughed and scooped him up, holding him close. These moments were so rare, she thought with a hint of sadness. The older Tommy got, the less he liked being held, coddled. And as Fiona had told her, the moments would become even fewer and farther between as he grew. So she treasured these moments, holding them close to her heart like a precious gift simply because she knew this would be her only child.

The thought no longer brought pain—at least, not the severe pain of the past. She'd learned long ago to accept things she couldn't change, and to accept whatever fate dealt her. She was far too practical to do anything else.

"So you're hungry then, too, is that it?" Bouncing him on her slender hip, she planted a loud, smacking kiss on his cheek, making him giggle, then wiped his mouth. "Looks like Grandma Fiona has been feeding you green Popsicles again."

She tried to smooth a hand through the knot of stickiness tangled in his hair, then gave up when he began to fuss, pushing her hands away.

"Hot dog," he repeated hopefully, giving her a charming, toothless smile.

Delighted, Brie laughed and gave him another kiss. "Son, you do have a one-track mind, especially when it comes to food."

He beamed, obviously taking her words as permission.

Craning his neck, the toddler's gaze landed on Patrick and he reached out one chubby hand to touch Patrick's face in curiosity.

Patrick froze, too stunned to react.

"Detective, this is my son, also known as the imp, Tommy McGee." Pride and love shone in her eyes, her face, her voice.

No, Patrick thought instantly, instinctively, unable to stop staring at the child.

That's my son.

And there was no denying it. The child was the mirror image of him at that age. His hair was an unruly black mop that fell forward over his eyes. And what eyes, Patrick thought. They were Sullivan blue, a shade unlike anything he'd ever seen except for family. And the boy had a dimple on the right sight of his face. Just like his brother Danny's.

Just like *his*.

If there was any doubt as to the child's true parentage, it had now been totally erased. This child had Sullivan blood running through him. One look was all he needed to recognize this child was his, and a Sullivan, through and through. From the coloring of his skin, to the color of his hair, to the unusual color of his eyes, right down to the family dimples at his mouth. Only his oldest brother Michael had escaped the curse of dimples, but that, Da had always explained, was simply because Michael was far too serious to allow something as frivolous as dimples in his life.

The reality of the moment hit Patrick like a ton of bricks.

My God, I have a child. A son.

A Sullivan.

His namesake.

Patrick could do little but stare. Logic, reason and speech seemed to have abandoned him. He could only feel and the feelings were so intense, so immediate, they nearly staggered him.

In the days since he'd received the letter, he'd thought about this moment, envisioned what he'd think, feel, but nothing had prepared him for the impact, for the immediate sense of rightness, of attachment, of...love.

He'd loved in his life, and loved well. His mother, father,

brothers, grandparents and a few times in his life he'd actually thought he loved a woman, but nothing had prepared him for *this* feeling that had swept over him the moment he'd laid eyes on his child.

His child.

A rash of emotions and thoughts raced through him and his heart ached for the tragedy that had touched and intertwined all their lives.

His son, this precious, innocent life, had been given away by an uncaring mother with no thought as to what the results of her actions would be on that child.

How would his son ever be able to understand his own flesh-and-blood mother had not wanted him and given him away?

And what of Brie McGee? A woman who had obviously wanted a child desperately. So much so, she had adopted a stranger's child and given herself and her love to him. And she did love him, Patrick realized with sudden relief. There was no mistaking the look of unmitigated joy and unabashed love on Brie's face the moment she'd laid eyes on her son.

And what about him?

A father who had been deprived of even the knowledge of his child. He'd lost two years of his son's life. Two precious years filled with irreplaceable moments that were forever lost to him.

He had to find a way, some way, to bring the three of them together and turn this tragedy into something positive so that his son would benefit from the knowledge that he was loved, was wanted by his father.

But how could he make Brie understand the circumstances, the need that had brought him here, and would keep him here until he'd accomplished what he set out to: to acknowledge and regain his son?

A great fear unlike anything Patrick had ever known swept over him. He knew how important a father was to a child—especially a boy; knew, too, what the lack of a father could do. He'd lived through it himself, knew how desolate and lonely it had made him feel. He had Da, yes, but it hadn't made up completely for the ache in his heart.

He remembered when he was eight, and on his first baseball team, they'd had a father-son pizza dinner. All the other kids had brought their fathers, and he'd watched and envied them.

Desolation.

That was what he most remembered from that night. He'd felt desolate and abandoned. Unable to shake the sadness that had seemed to wrap around his eight-year-old heart as he watched the other boys and their fathers laugh, play and enjoy each other.

As he grew older, he understood logically that it wasn't his father's fault that he'd been prematurely killed in the line of duty. But at eight, he hadn't been very logical. Only desperately needy for the father he no longer had and missed terribly. And so he let the anger build for the man who was no longer in his life.

At night sometimes, he would lie awake in the darkness, imagining he could hear his father's footsteps or his booming laugh. He'd creep out of bed and down the stairs, only to realize that he'd been dreaming.

His father was never coming home again.

It had taken him a long time to accept and an even longer time to understand. He still wasn't certain he understood it completely.

But he remembered the feelings; they were etched in the corners of his heart.

He never wanted his son to look at other boys, other fathers and feel that desperate need, that hungry envy for what others had. It was an overwhelming feeling for a child. It had always made him feel…different than everyone else. Somehow…inferior. He couldn't explain it, not even now as an adult, but it was a feeling he'd never been able to talk about, not with anyone, not even the family.

He had no idea if his brothers Michael or Danny had ever felt that way; he'd never know because he'd never ask them. To do so would seem disloyal to his grandfather and all the years of love and dedication Da had given to him.

But still, having Da was not the same as having his father.

Suddenly Patrick realized his biggest fear was never to be given the opportunity to be a father, dooming his own son to the same feelings of doubt and envy that he had suffered from for so many years.

Looking at his child, his son, Patrick knew without a doubt he could never, ever allow that to happen. He'd make sure it never happened.

Tommy turned to Patrick with outstretched arms and a wide, angelic grin. "Hot dog?"

Shaking her head at her child's antics, Brie smiled, stroking a hand down her son's head. "Tommy McGee, you're not to be begging food from strangers like some piker."

Totally besotted by his son, Patrick looked at Brie. "May I?" He held out his arms, which had never seemed so empty before.

"He doesn't usually go to strangers, especially men," she commented hesitantly, a frown knitting her brow. But apparently her son was going to go to *this* stranger, she thought with some surprise as her son leaned toward Patrick, arms outstretched, nearly toppling himself out of her arms in an effort to get into Patrick's.

Patrick rescued the tot, lifting him under the arms and swinging him up on his hip, making the boy giggle again.

"So it's a hot dog you're after, huh?" Patrick asked with a grin of his own. His son smelled of baby powder and sweetness. He was certain he'd never smelled anything quite so wonderful.

Brie brushed a wayward strand of hair off her cheek. "He goes through cycles where his taste buds feast on the same thing for weeks at a time." Brie smiled and reached out to smooth her son's T-shirt down. "It's hot dogs this week." She rolled her eyes. "Last week it was peanut butter."

"Pea butter?" Grinning hopefully, Tommy raised one sticky, chubby fisted hand to Patrick's face. "Hot dog?" he caroled again. Kicking his chubby legs, he patted his sticky hands against Patrick's face as if he were playing patty-cake against his cheeks, making Patrick laugh.

"Do you have children, Detective?" Brie asked, watching his face as he watched her child. Even though he was smiling, he had an odd, wistful look about him. Almost sad, she thought. Something had hurt him, she realized. Something dreadful if she was any judge. She wondered if it had something to do with a child. Perhaps that would explain the way he'd looked at her son.

She had to admit, he certainly had a way about him with children. Tommy usually never went to anyone he didn't know, especially men, but he seemed totally comfortable with the detective.

Curious now, she looked at her son, his hair so dark, his eyes so blue, then her gaze shifted to Patrick, and for a moment she merely stared, as something cold and foreboding swept over her and touched her heart. Her hands began to tremble, and she slipped them in her pockets, cursing herself for her foolishness.

"Children?" Patrick repeated, engrossed in the sticky little hands touching his face. His gaze shifted to Brie and he realized she was staring at him with mild curiosity and a bit of fear. "No...Yes...I mean..." His voice trailed off sheepishly.

His words had her brow lifting in surprise. "Yes? No? Not certain if you have children, Detective?" She shook her head. Apparently the man was not just daft, but forgetful as well. "And what of a wife? Perhaps she knows for sure if you've a babe or two lying about?" She tried not to grin, but it slipped past her.

Patrick shook his head, shifting his son higher on his hip. "A wife?" he repeated dully, feeling a bit nervous by her questions. With his attention divided, Patrick shook his head. "No, I'm...uh...not married."

"I see. You're not married, but you're not quite certain if you have wee ones or not. Have I got this right, Detective?"

"Uh...right." He knew he sounded like a blathering idiot, but he couldn't help it. How could he be expected to answer questions intelligently, while coming face-to-face with his own flesh and blood for the first time? He was lucky he was able to breathe and stand up at the same time, considering how he was feeling.

It hit him again, the emotions that had been lying so close to the surface since he'd received the letter. His son was looking at him with such trust, such...innocence, he wanted to gather him close to his heart and hold him in his protective embrace forever.

Now, for the first time, he understood perhaps what his mother had gone through for so many years. She'd told him once that having a child changed your life and your priorities forever. It also, she'd advised, changed your heart.

He hadn't understood at the time, couldn't understand since he'd had no experience. But now, holding his child in his arms, understanding came quickly.

Sighing, Fiona bustled toward them, arms outstretched. "Let me get the child his hot dog before he pesters the daylights out of everyone."

Reluctantly, Patrick released his hold, handing over his son to the older woman, but not before the child had planted a soft, sticky kiss on his cheek.

"Come on, luv," Fiona cooed to the toddler. "Let's get you a hot dog and you can sit and watch 'Sesame Street.'"

"Street?"

"Yes, luv." Fiona couldn't resist. She pressed her lips to his forehead.

Tommy beamed at her, patting both hands against her cheeks. "Big Bird?"

"Yes, luv, and Oscar the Grouch as well, although why you watch the Grouch on TV when you've got your own Grandma Grouch right here is a mystery."

"The Grouch," Tommy caroled loudly, making her laugh. He peeked over Fiona's shoulder, and lifted chubby arms to wave. "Bye-bye," he called, frantically waving his hands in the air. "Bye-bye."

Patrick lifted a hand, his eyes longingly following his son. "Bye-bye." He felt as if someone was cutting out his heart with a rusty knife.

"Detective?"

His gaze shifted back to Brie and he noted there was a hint of shadowy fear in her eyes.

"Yes?"

Her gaze was steady on his and she crossed her arms across her breasts to stave off the wicked chill that had suddenly invaded her bones. Chill and fear, a fear so deep it seemed to have rattled her heart loose in her chest. She tried to keep the anxiety out of her voice, tried not to show the emotions she was feeling. Nervous, she licked her lips, tilting her head back to meet his gaze fully.

"Just exactly who are you?" she whispered.

Chapter Three

"Is there somewhere more private we can talk?" Patrick asked quietly.

Trying to retain her composure and keep her sudden fear under control, Brie took a deep, shaky breath. "Of course." She glanced around as if she'd never seen her showroom before. Her nerves were squealing in such alarm, it was difficult to think, to make her body move. "In the back. My office...it's in the back."

Patrick took her arm and followed her to the back office, where he gently closed the door behind him. Quickly he took the room in. It was decorated in beautiful shades of green and pink, with definite feminine touches. The walls were a deep green striped wallpaper, edged with a matching pink-and-green border. The floor was planked oak with an Oriental throw rug, which picked up the colors on the walls. There was a small Queen Anne's desk dead center; the top was meticulously neat except for a small pile of folders standing in one corner. A large oak swivel chair was tucked into the middle of the desk. One corner boasted a large pink and green striped Queen Anne chair. In the other corner sat a small, portable playpen with a various assortment of toys in it. The sight of it made him smile.

This might be an office, but there was also room for a child. He liked that. Clearly, Sabrina McGee took her mothering role seriously. It pleased him.

The moment the door clicked closed Brie whirled on him, studying him. She took a quick breath of air, the way one might in order to prepare for an unplanned jump into a very icy lake.

"Detective." She couldn't keep the fear out of her voice. "I want to know who you are, and I want to know right now." Pressing a hand to her tummy, she tried to calm her nerves.

Patrick hesitated for only a moment, then pulled the letter from the attorney as well as the crumbled lavender letter from Barbara from his pocket and quietly handed them to her. She looked at him for a long, silent moment before reaching for the letters.

He wasn't certain this was the way he would have liked to handle this, but he'd always believed in playing the hand he'd been dealt. His own heart was pounding in his chest as she took the letters from him.

With shaky hands, Brie unfolded the letters, grabbed her reading glasses off her desk and began reading.

"My God." Her hand went to her mouth and her legs would have gone out from under her if Patrick hadn't caught her arm, guiding her toward the plush chair in the corner. She didn't look up at him, didn't even acknowledge his presence or his touch as she continued reading the letter that would forever alter all their lives.

Brie's mind tried hard to comprehend what she was reading. She knew of Barbara Keats, of course. She had met with Barbara during the final stages of the woman's pregnancy. The adoption had been handled privately, discreetly, through their attorneys, and now that very same attorney who had represented Barbara's interests had sent Patrick Sullivan the letter. She remembered his name.

But, according to this letter—if it was authentic— Tommy's mother had lied to them. She'd told them Tommy's father was deceased, which was why she was giving her child up. She'd explained that as a single woman she didn't feel she could give a child the right kind of upbringing.

But Tommy's father wasn't dead; he was very much alive, and standing right in front of her.

Dear God.

It couldn't be possible.

But it was, Brie realized with the deep-bedded female instinct she'd possessed all her life and now no longer questioned. In her heart of hearts, Brie knew that Barbara Keats might have lied before. She dared a glance at Patrick, her heart sinking. But now, Brie realized, Barbara Keats had finally told the truth.

Patrick Sullivan was the boy's biological father.

And she didn't know what to do about it.

So many thoughts, emotions swirled through Brie, but none stronger than the fear that nearly overwhelmed her. Tommy was all she had left in the world. She couldn't even comprehend that perhaps she could lose him. Not now. Not ever.

Her eyes swam and her hands shook. Aware that the detective was still watching her, she didn't bother to wipe the tears as they cascaded down her face. She didn't seem to have the energy. Fear had robbed her of strength.

She finished reading Barbara's letter, then read it again, forcing herself to take deep breaths. When she was finished, she handed it back to him without a word.

Long silent moments passed. It was so quiet, so still, the sound of their breathing echoed loudly in the room.

"What do you want?" she finally whispered, lifting a hand to dash at her tears. In an instant, her safe secure world had shattered into a million frightening, fragmented pieces and she had nothing safe, nothing strong to cling to.

Patrick took a deep breath, dragging a shaky hand through his hair. "What I didn't want, and didn't plan to do, was scare you." Guilt ate at him. He could see the real fear on her face which had paled, and not regained its color. Her hands were trembling and her eyes were red from the tears which slipped heedlessly down her face. He had a sudden urge to hold her, to protect her, and then he realized that would be futile, for what he would be protecting her from was...himself.

"Too late for that, Detective Sullivan." Her voice was eerily soft. She dared a glance at him and saw the real pain in his eyes. But she couldn't sympathize with him. He was the enemy; a man who had the ability to rob her of the only thing that meant anything to her in life. Her son.

"How long...how long have you known about...us?" she whispered.

"About ten days," he said softly. "And I must admit, I was as shocked as you are."

She nodded. "I see." She tried to think of him, of his feelings when he'd learned he had a child he knew nothing about. It must have been devastating. But at the moment she couldn't think about him or his loss. She could only think of the *danger* he represented to her.

"And what is it you planned to do about it now that you know?"

She dared a glance at him, deciding it was best to know immediately what his intentions were. She'd always believed in facing bad news head-on. She might be a woman alone, but she was no pushover. She'd learned at an early age to stand up for herself and her loved ones.

She didn't give him a chance to answer. She took a deep breath, pressing her hand deeper against her tummy, hoping to hold on to her lunch a bit longer.

"If you've come on some misguided notion that you're going to claim Tommy, I can tell you right now, I'll fight you." She surged to her feet. Fire flashed in her eyes and her chin lifted with determination. "He's my son, has been my son from the moment they laid him in my arms. I've loved him, cared for him, reared him. He knows no other home, no other mother, and I'll not let his world be tossed upside down by anyone, not even you."

Her tone of voice, so firm, so…final immediately irritated him and Patrick tried with admirable determination to hang on to his own temper.

"I don't recall making any statements about taking him away from you."

It had crossed his mind several times, especially after talking to his cousin Peter about what his legal rights were in this case. Normally he would have none. But the fact that he'd never known about the child gave him some legal recourse.

In the state of Illinois, a biological father had thirty days to make a claim to his child. Thirty days. But the hitch was the thirty days began from the time the father learned of the child's birth. He hadn't learned of his child until ten days ago. He'd been deprived of the ability to exercise his rights by his lack of knowledge. Now that he knew, he could, if he wanted, exercise his rights and possibly overturn the adoption of his son and gain total custody. There was already legal precedence in Illinois, a fact in his favor.

But he wasn't entirely convinced that was the best course of action for his son. The child had known no other mother than Brie McGee. No other life or family. Patterns and history had already been set. To yank Tommy from all that was familiar might be far too damaging to him. And Patrick wouldn't do that to the boy. His son's welfare came first, even before his own desperate needs and desires to claim his son.

Brie stared at him, her eyes hard, challenging. "And what proof do I have that you are indeed Tommy's biological father?" Agitated, she paced the small room, her mind spinning with fear. "You're a perfect stranger to me. You come in and show me a letter supposedly written by a lawyer and the child's mother and expect me to take at face value that you are my son's father?" Still pacing, she splayed her hands. "You have no proof. I've only your word, which, excuse me for saying, means absolutely nothing to me since I know nothing about you nor do I have any reason to believe you are who you say you are."

"I think the letter speaks for itself," he pointed out, struggling to hold on to his own surging emotions. "Surely you can't think a lawyer would be a party to some kind of fraud?"

"The letter means nothing," she spat out, whirling on him, desperately grasping at straws. "Merely words on paper. And as for the lawyer, I believe even men of the law can be persuaded to do things they wouldn't ordinarily for the right price."

Patrick couldn't help it, the absurdity of the situation struck him and he laughed. The sound was harsh and bitter. "Brie, be reasonable. Why on earth would I want to claim a child that wasn't mine? Why would I want to accept the legal, moral or financial responsibility? What possible reason or motive would I have?"

"I don't…know." She didn't want to admit that he had a point; that his question made absolute perfect sense. What reason, indeed? The knowledge only fueled her anger and fear.

How could he expect her to be reasonable when he'd walked into her life and tossed it upside down?

"I have no reason to believe either letter is real, nor do I have any reason to believe one is truly from Tommy's biological mother." Brie faced him, ready to go toe-to-toe with the devil if it meant protecting her child. "Do not mistake me for a simpering fool, Detective Sullivan. Make no mistake, I was raised to protect mine, and Tommy is mine, pure and simple, and there's nothing you can say or do that can ever change that."

Patrick shifted his frame, struggling to hold on to his temper. "You haven't given me much time to say much of anything. You've been doing all the talking," he added, making her flush. His voice changed, then hardened. "In fact, you've done nothing but tell me what you're going to do and not going to do. You haven't even given me a chance to explain why I'm here."

Properly chastised, she nodded, taking a deep breath. She'd always had a flash fire temper; it had been a curse since childhood. But she wouldn't defend it simply because she'd learned long ago she was a woman of deep emotions, and no amount of scolding had been able to bank them. So she'd just accepted them and lived with them. And the consequences.

"Fine, then," she said on a slow breath, giving him her full attention and crossing her arms across her breasts to ward off the chill that had invaded her body and her spirit. "Explain then."

Patrick waited a beat, merely watching her. Whatever had been humming between them in the display room, vibrated even stronger now, fueled no doubt by the confines of the room and the heat of their tempers. It was primitive and basic, and only added to his wariness.

He didn't want to acknowledge that in spite of the awkward circumstances he was drawn to this woman in a way that seemed altogether too natural and instinctive. He didn't want to admit that he found her fascinating and beautiful. All fiery temper and passions.

The loyalty that simmered from her was something he understood. Being a Sullivan, that type of loyalty had been bred in him, and all his family. It was a rare commodity he'd found in few others.

Family was the center of his life, and apparently the center of hers. The knowledge softened his heart toward her and he felt a rise of compassion.

"Brie." He couldn't resist, he reached out and laid a gentle hand on her pale cheek, wanting to know if that skin was as soft as it looked. It was. His thumb began a slow caress, warming her tender skin, making him wonder if she was that soft all over.

He banished the thought, unwilling to allow anything to interfere with his objective. As drawn as he was to this woman, he couldn't become blind to reality. A beautiful woman had already lied and deceived him, causing him to almost lose his son.

He couldn't allow another woman to blind him, especially *this* woman who had the ultimate power over his son.

He wouldn't be a fool a second time. Not for this woman or any woman, not when the welfare of his child was at stake.

Still, he continued to watch her, to caress that soft skin, drawn by a power far stronger than his resolve. He thought she'd shrink back, pull away, but she didn't. Her eyes merely widened and he saw a flash of emotion again. It was something he couldn't identify. Her cheeks were still damp with tears, and using his thumb, he caressed the silky softness, brushing the dampness away.

"I know this has been a shock—" One brow rose as she opened her mouth to say something, then snapped it shut quickly. It amused him, but he went on. "But you have to understand what a shock it was for me." He shook his dark head, wanting—needing—to explain. "I would never, *never* have allowed my child, my son, my own flesh and blood, to be given away. The idea is totally inconceivable—"

"But it's done, Detective," she said softly, wishing she had the strength to step away from his touch. Wishing the haunting sadness in his voice didn't tug at her heart. He was hurting as well, she realized, but she couldn't allow herself to feel for him. Not now. Not ever. She had a child to protect. Her child.

She made the mistake of glancing up at Patrick, of seeing the actual pain in those glorious blue eyes. Her breath withered, and she felt the tug on her heart as surely as if someone had attached a rope to it and pulled.

Unconsciously she nestled her face against the soft, gentleness of his hand, astounded that she could welcome his touch of comfort, knowing he needed the comfort as well.

They were both hurting, she realized. Caught in a web of pain and deceit neither had had any control over. Drawn together against their wills by tragic circumstances that would forever alter their lives.

And Tommy's.

The fear rose again, almost to a panic, and Brie hated to admit it, but at this moment, his touch of comfort was more welcome and necessary than she could ever admit.

Perhaps because it had been so long since she'd been touched or comforted, especially by a man, and at the moment she was so terribly frightened. The fact that he was the cause of her fear only added to her distress over her attraction to him. It was almost a betrayal of her own body. Her mind knew he was a danger, the ultimate threat, yet her body was responding in a way that had nothing to do with fear, and everything to do with her being a woman, and he, a man.

"Yes," Patrick said on a long sigh. "It's done, Brie. But because something was done without my knowledge, does it mean I should be punished for the rest of my life? Deprived of my child?" He rushed on at the look of pure panic on her face. "And should my son be punished for something he had no control over? Should you doom that wonderful little boy to a life without the benefit of a loving father simply because of the selfish act of a foolish woman?"

Stunned, she merely stared at him. She'd been so caught up in her own feelings, she hadn't thought about Tommy. Dear Lord, the little imp. She loved him so.

How many times had she longed and prayed and wished for Dennis to be a father to Tommy? A true father? The way her own father had been to her? But it was never to be. Dennis had a cold heart, and he'd rejected the helpless little child who had wanted nothing more than his love.

It had broken her heart. She had blamed herself, and suffered the guilt, knowing it was her fault her own husband couldn't accept their child. Her fault, Tommy was forever doomed not to have a father. It had been Dennis's way of punishing her for going against his wishes, for wanting a child, even if it wasn't of their own blood.

No, Tommy had never been *theirs*. Only hers. Always. Dennis had made that clear. While he hadn't been deliberately cruel to the child, he had made it clear he wanted no part in the child's life. It was a burden and a pain she carried in her heart, always desperately trying to make it up to Tommy, trying to be both mother and father to him.

She truly believed that a child needed a father; she remembered how important her own father had been to her life, her development. She couldn't even imagine what her life would have been like without the man she had loved as no other. Her father had always been there for her, the steady rock to cling to throughout all of life's storms. In spite of the fact that she'd had a cold, vengeful mother who had made it clear she didn't want a daughter, her father had always made her feel loved, wanted, special. It was a feeling she had treasured throughout her lifetime. Losing her father was something she had still not gotten over, even though it had been almost ten years. The thought of him brought another flash of tears simply because the loss was still so fresh. And oh, how her father would have loved the little imp!

"And what will you tell Tommy when he's older and he questions why he doesn't have a father like the other kids?" Patrick went on, his gaze searching her face. "Will you tell him he had a father, one who wanted to be part of his life, but you forbade it because of your own fears and selfishness?"

She flinched, almost making him regret his words. Almost. His words were harsh, and he knew it, but he had no choice. He had to make her understand how important this was to him. To them. All of them.

"Don't you think when he knows you deprived him of a father, he will resent you? Perhaps turn on you for depriving him of something every little boy needs?"

Oh, God, she couldn't even bear the thought. She remembered something her father had always told her. *Be careful what you wish for.* Hadn't she wished for a father for her son?

Well, now that she had her wish, she only prayed it would not end up costing her her son.

"I love him," she said simply. Her eyes swam and she couldn't stop the tears. "Tommy's all I have," she whispered. "I wouldn't know what to do without him." She couldn't bear the thought; it was almost a physical pain, as if someone was squeezing her heart, draining the life from it.

From the beginning she'd always known there was a risk with adoption. But she'd been so desperate for a child, so desperate to fill her arms to make up for the emptiness in her belly and in her heart that she'd blocked any thought of complications from her mind.

She'd been so careful. She thought she'd made the right decision, choosing a mother who couldn't provide for her child, and one who had no husband or boyfriend to contend with. It had seemed like an ideal situation.

Why hadn't she probed deeper? she wondered now with deep regret. She knew why, but couldn't face it. Dennis had not wanted another man's child. He'd blamed her for being barren, then resisted when she'd wanted to adopt, unable to love a child not of his blood. It had caused a rift in their already failing marriage. Eventually he'd gone along with the adoption only because she'd been so insistent about it. She'd wanted it so desperately to the exclusion of everything else, thinking that once they'd had a child in the house, his heart would soften.

She'd been wrong. So wrong.

She'd fallen in love with the baby on sight. It didn't matter that he was not borne of her body; he was borne of her heart, and she could not love him more if she had given birth to him.

Dennis had turned out to be a man from the old school with a cold heart, and had he not passed on, she would have left him. She'd not tie herself to a man again. Ever. Never again would she subject herself to a man who believed her to be nothing but chattel, a possession of his with no thoughts or dreams or desires of her own. A man who dictated her life, with no thought to her happiness. A man whom she'd come to need, trust, love and depend on, only to be betrayed and disappointed.

Nay, one marriage in a lifetime was enough. She would never allow another man to make her feel inferior because she couldn't have children, nor would she allow any man to ever hurt the child she did have.

Not even his own father.

No, she'd learned her lesson once, and she would not go through that grief and pain ever again. She had her son and her shop and that was all she'd ever need or want. It was enough to fill her life and her heart, and she had no room for a man, especially another cold, selfish man.

"I'd rather die than lose my son." Her voice caught on a sob, and Patrick didn't think, he merely gathered her stiff body close, holding her in his arms, wanting to comfort her, knowing how painful this was for her.

And for him.

In spite of their relative sizes she fit perfectly against him, his chin resting just at the top of her red hair. He tried not to think of her sweet, female scent which wafted between them, tickling his senses, intoxicating his mind. He tried not to think of how right she felt in his arms.

Holding her against him, he became vividly aware of the softness of her curves, and his body's instinctive response to a sweet-smelling, soft female body.

He felt her slender shoulders shake as sobs shook her, and he merely gathered her closer, wanting to ease her pain.

She was close enough for her scent to infiltrate his every breath, to seep into his pores and his heart, making him want to ease the growing need that had flared to life the moment he'd touched her.

All the protective instincts inside rose rapidly to the surface, making him tighten his arms around her. Guilt swamped him. He knew he'd shocked her, hurt her, and it wasn't his way. Sullivan men were raised with a healthy respect for women; he and his brothers had been taught that women were to be loved, taken care of, cherished. How many times had Da told him that a man didn't prove his manhood with fists or strength? But with gentleness and love?

Emotions warred with logic, and Patrick tried hard to keep his feelings in perspective. It was only natural that he feel the need to comfort, he reasoned, since he was the one responsible for her tears, her fears. He'd never meant to hurt Brie. He'd merely wanted to protect his rights and his son.

"Knowing I'd already lost him almost killed me," he whispered, unable to resist stroking the long length of her back, knowing this woman above all others would understand. "He's my child." Patrick didn't know if he could ever express the torment he'd gone through since he'd received the letters.

Brie sniffled and clutched the front of his shirt. Her pulse had jumped, then skittered the moment he'd pulled her into his arms and her naturally cautious resolve around men melted. His chest was broad and seemed meant as a resting place for her weary, pounding head. Greedily accepting the comfort he so generously offered, Brie let loose a heartfelt sigh, allowing herself to indulge in this moment of pleasure.

Patrick Sullivan was a dangerous man, she realized. Apparently dangerous to her heart as well as her life, but she couldn't seem to back away from him. Some latent need for comfort during this terrible moment of truth forced her to stay. And then she realized sadly just how long it had been since she'd felt the comfort of a man during an emotional storm. Too long. Her heart had been battered, bruised and broken by an uncaring man who had hardened his heart to her and her child.

But this man, Patrick Sullivan, was apparently caring, kind and comforting. And she was ashamed to admit that in spite of the dire circumstances, she was drawn to him much the same way a child is drawn to the bright, dangerous flames of a fire.

Only to get burned.

Patrick Sullivan could always ruin her life and snatch the one thing in the world that mattered to her. She couldn't forget that.

But she also couldn't forget that he was the first man to have shown her a bit of kindness, of tenderness, of comfort, in many, many years. And she realized she was starved for this man's touch. Starved in a way she'd not thought possible until this moment.

She should have been ashamed for needing his comfort, but she wasn't. She was too overwhelmed by fear, by the enormous complications this situation presented.

"I...I guess I should feel some compassion for you." She sniffled, trying to ignore his very potent male scent. It was strong, clean and so totally masculine, she rubbed her nose against his soft shirt, allowing the scent to entice her. "Some understanding for what you've gone through. Never knowing you had a son until now. But I can't." Her voice broke on a sob, and she shook her head, ashamed that she couldn't even afford him that small bit of humanity. She felt small for it, but couldn't help it. "Not yet. I can only feel the threat that your presence has brought to my life. And to Tommy's."

Emotions warred within her. She wanted to cling to his

strength, to savor his embrace, but as much as she needed to now more than any other time in her life, she knew she couldn't.

He was the enemy. A man who could take from her the only thing that mattered. She had to remember that and keep her own needs under control.

Aye, she might still be a woman with womanly feelings and emotions, but she was also a mother. And from the moment they'd laid her precious babe in her arms, Tommy and his needs had come first. Anything and everything else would always be secondary.

She would do nothing to jeopardize her son's well-being.

Nothing.

Especially where this man was concerned.

No matter what he offered.

"I understand your fears," he said. And he did. In spite of his own tumultuous emotions, he understood exactly how she felt and how fearful she was.

With his arms still around her, with her body pressed closed to his, he looked down at her just as she looked up and he felt as if a bad-tempered mule had just landed a foot right in his gut.

Her eyes widened, then grew wary. He felt her stiffen a bit, and the look of surprise and the twin spots of color that etched her cheeks told him she was as vividly aware of him and the elemental tension simmering between them as he was. It could be a monumental complication, Patrick realized. It should have annoyed him.

It pleased him.

Staring up at him, at those beautiful blue eyes, so familiar, so like her son's, Brie felt her breath catch as her heart seemed to stall and her thoughts all but scattered. She was pressed tightly against him, his arms gently holding her. He was so close, his warm, sweet breath fanned her skin, making her want to curl even closer to him. Staring up into his eyes, those sad, beautiful eyes, she felt something powerful soften her battered heart.

When she looked into his face, she saw her son.

His son.

She tried to take a breath, but she couldn't seem to manage it. It was as if someone had drained the room of air. She just kept staring at him, letting her gaze search his face, finally settling on his mouth. It was lush, full and looked unbearably soft. She wondered what that mouth would taste like, feel like, pressed against hers. The thought caused a bout of panic, and she tried to step back, but Patrick held her gently, refusing to let her back away.

"Brie." Her name came out a husky whisper, surprising both of them. Brie's heart was thudding so loudly in her chest, she feared he might hear it. Her palms grew damp, her knees weak, and she was grateful for his strength, for if he wasn't holding her she feared she might collapse.

Perhaps it was just the shock of his announcement and the circumstances that had brought them together, she reasoned, unwilling to admit that she was having such a powerful reaction to this man. Yes, that was all it was, she decided. Surely it was nothing to worry about.

Patrick couldn't resist sliding a hand up and down her slender back, feeling the gentle slope of her delicate spine, knowing he was treading in dangerous water, but unable to stop himself.

"We've both had a shock, Brie, but shock or not, now we have to deal with the reality of the situation."

Reality. The word reverberated dully in her mind. She wasn't certain she was up to dealing with reality at the moment. She was far too fearful, far too frustrated and far too flustered by this man.

She nodded hesitantly, lifting her chin to stare at him,

trying to ignore the conflicting emotions in her heart. His eyes, she thought again, were so much like Tommy's. But they bore such pain it made her heart ache. Her eyes slid closed for a moment as she battled the softening of her heart. She couldn't allow herself to feel sympathy for him. She couldn't allow him to know that she understood how he felt, knew how she'd feel if she'd been robbed of her son. It was a tragedy that they'd all found themselves in. But what was to be done about it now? She wasn't certain she could face the answer. Wasn't certain she wanted to hear the reality.

Finally she took a deep shaky breath.

"All right, Detective." She licked her suddenly dry lips and watched his eyes follow the movement of her tongue, making her skin flush as if it had been caressed. "I'm willing to listen."

His own emotions were in turmoil, and Patrick tried to think on a rational level, but it was hard to be rational when his body was responding in a way that was nearly making thought impossible.

"I think...I think we can agree that we both want what's best for our son..."

Our son. His words had the effect of a bucket of cold water, making her shiver. Gathering her strength, Brie shook her head, then stepped back and out of his arms, wanting to put some much needed distance between them.

Patrick Sullivan made her want things she knew she could never have.

Be careful what you wish for.

She could hear her father's deep voice whispering in her ear, and immediately she returned to her senses.

"Our son," she whispered with a sad shake of her head. "That will take some getting used to. Tommy has always

been *my* son. Just mine.'' Hadn't Dennis reminded her of
that each and every day?

Although her statement struck him as odd, given that
she'd shared Tommy with her husband, Patrick chose not
to pursue it at the moment. Right now he had far more
important things on his mind.

''Brie, I think we need to agree on a few things right up
front, before we go any further.'' He took a breath, wondering why he felt so bereft now that she wasn't in his
arms. ''As his parents, I think we need to agree that we
don't want Tommy hurt.''

Our.

We.

He kept using words that connected them in a way she
found threatening on many, many levels.

''No, of course not,'' Brie agreed quietly, lacing her
hands together to stop their trembling.

''Nor do we want to frighten or disrupt his life, or shake
his stability or security in any way, correct?'' He watched
her carefully.

She nodded, unable to pull her gaze from his. ''Aye, as
his mother I can't allow that.''

Relief flooded him, knowing she was the kind of mother
who would do anything to protect her child. If he'd doubted
her love, her devotion to the child, all he had to do was
remember the glorious look on her face when she'd looked
at the boy.

''Nor would I want it.'' With a sigh, Patrick dragged his
hand through his hair. ''I didn't come here to hurt either
of you, Brie. I came merely because I want a chance to get
to know my son, to be part of his life.''

''I...can understand that,'' she admitted, then frowned.
''But I don't particularly like it.''

She didn't want him in their lives; he was a threat, would

always be a threat to her and her son's security and stability. Not to mention the threat he suddenly represented to her heart. She'd never thought she'd ever have feelings for another man, certain Dennis's coldness and cruelty had killed that part of her. Perhaps because she'd believed herself dead inside for so long, the discovery that she was very much alive and very much capable of having…female feelings for a man, was very threatening on a whole other level.

No, she didn't want Patrick Sullivan in her life for many reasons, but there was nothing she could do about it now. He was here, the deed was done and now she'd have to make the best of what was to come, and simply guard her son and her heart in the process.

"Whether you like it or not, Brie, he has a right to know he has a father, and I have a right to be part of his life. He is *my* son," he added softly, wanting his objective to be very, very clear. "And I have every intention of exercising my parental rights legally or any other way necessary."

He wanted his son to be part of the Sullivans, to know of his kin and his clan. To know he was loved and wanted. The fact that Patrick hadn't known about the child's birth in no way diminished his need to claim the child as his own. As it should be.

"Legally?" A shaft of fear arrowed through Brie, striking her heart and sending shivers up and down her spine. She merely stared at him, stunned.

"If necessary." Though his words were firm, his voice was deliberately gentle. "I'm hoping that won't be necessary. I'm hoping *you* won't make that necessary." His eyes bore into hers, making her breath catch again. "It's your decision, Brie. Entirely yours. We can do this the easy way or the hard way. But make no mistake, I *will* be part of the child's life. *My* child." He reached for her hands and noted they were cold, trembling.

"Brie?" He waited for her to look up at him. She was nibbling on her lower lip, struggling not to cry. The sight brought a pain unlike any he'd ever known. The protective urge to comfort, to hold was so strong, so fierce, he simply had to bank it. He could not allow anything to interfere or shadow the reason for his presence.

Especially not something as simple as attraction, although there appeared to be nothing simple about the feelings this woman immediately aroused in him. They were strong, irrepressible and compelling, causing desire to flare inside.

But he couldn't be sidetracked.

He'd simply ignore the impact this beautiful woman was having on him. Ignore it, and remember that she was a woman capable of depriving him of the most important thing in his life. Just as another woman had already done.

"I'm not asking you to give up Tommy, I'm merely asking you to share him. With me."

Brie nodded in silent relief, grateful for at least this little bit he was giving her. She had no idea what she would have done if he had demanded she turn Tommy over to him.

"I appreciate that, Patrick." She had to force the words out. "You realize I'll need to verify you are indeed Tommy's biological father, and that all you've told me is true." Lifting a hand, she rubbed a throbbing spot on her temple.

"Of course." Patrick nodded toward the letter which had drifted to the floor after she'd read it. "Although I can't imagine you needing any more proof than that."

"No," Brie insisted with a shake of her head. "It's not enough. Barbara lied to me once. Certainly she could lie about who the boy's real father was. I'll want a blood test to be certain."

"Fine." He'd give her all his blood if necessary. He didn't care what he had to do to prove he was Tommy's biological father. "But I can assure you I'm the boy's father." Blood test or not, one look at the child had been more proof than necessary. Patrick reached in his pocket and extracted his wallet.

He handed Brie a picture.

She stared at it for a moment, then frowned. "How... how..." She shook her head, then glanced up at him in total confusion. "How did you get a picture of Tommy?" She shook her head again, trying to shake loose the cobwebs. "And who are these other boys?" She peered closer at the picture, making Patrick smile.

"It's not Tommy," he said quietly. "It's me. He's the spitting image of me at that age. And those other boys are my brothers, Michael and Danny. That picture was taken on my second birthday."

A shiver ran over Brie as she continued to stare at the picture. Patrick and Tommy could have been twins, they looked so much alike, she realized, her heart sinking even farther.

She glanced at Patrick again, and remembered the eerie feelings she'd gotten when he'd held Tommy in his arms. The resemblance was so strong, it was a wonder she hadn't guessed immediately.

"Brie, I know this has been unsettling for you, but I don't have a lot of time or patience at the moment. I feel cheated, robbed of some of the most precious moments of my son's young life. His birthdays, his first step, his first word." Something caught in Patrick's throat and he had to swallow hard. "I don't want to miss another moment with my son." He shifted his weight, and his eyes darkened. "Do you understand?" His gaze searched hers, saw her confusion, her uncertainty, and his resolve strengthened, hardening his heart. "And I don't intend to let anyone prevent me from missing another day or another moment with him."

His blue eyes bore into hers, and she felt another shiver track over her skin.

"Not even you." His voice was cool and calm. "*Especially* you. Like it or not, Brie, you'd better get used to me. I'm here to stay."

Chapter Four

"Ma-ma cry?" Snuggled on Brie's lap, dressed in a pair of "Sesame Street" footed pajamas, Tommy patted her damp cheeks with both hands, then pressed his nose against hers, bright blue eyes wide and curious as they stared directly into hers. "Cry, Ma-ma?"

Smiling in spite of her tears, Brie gathered her son closer, trying to ease his fears.

"No, sweetheart," she lied, sniffling and forcing herself to smile. "Mama's not crying."

"Wet!" he declared, patting her cheek again, and bouncing on his knees in her lap. "Wet! Wet!" Each little word was punctuated with a pat to her cheeks, making her wonder why she'd ever taught him to play patty-cake.

Despite her little fib, not to mention the heartache and panic tearing at her, Brie found herself smiling in genuine pleasure; her child never failed to lift her spirits and soothe her heart.

"Come here, sweetheart." Cradling him close in her arms, she buried her nose in the thick, chubby folds of his neck, inhaling deeply of his sweet baby scent, sighing in genuine pleasure for the first time today.

"Ma-ma rock?" Tommy wiggled in her arms, getting comfortable as she pressed a foot to the floor to set the rocker in motion.

This was their quiet time. Hers and Tommy's. A time when she answered no phones or doorbells, nor did she allow anything or anyone to interfere. This was time she devoted exclusively to her son.

Every night since she'd brought Tommy home, she'd rocked him to sleep. It was as much for his comfort and pleasure as hers. A small ritual that brought a calm, peaceful end to each busy day; a ritual that fed her wounded heart and nourished her famished soul.

Watching Tommy's eyes droop, Brie smiled, then glanced around. The living room was bathed in a muted golden glow. The lights were out, except for the bright flickering flames in the fireplace, and several scented candles lit around the room. It was only early October and yet the wind howled at the windows, reminding her that winter was coming.

"Sing, Ma-ma?" he mumbled. He pulled his thumb out of his mouth only long enough to get the words out. "Sing?"

His request brought a smile to her face as his free hand reached out and snagged the front of her blouse. He clutched it tightly in his chubby little fist as she began to croon softly to him, a sad, old Irish ballad her father used to sing to her.

Somehow, singing it to Tommy always made her feel as if her son and her late father were somehow connected. It brought her a bit of peace, and right now, peace was something she sorely needed.

Brie shook her head, still shell-shocked from the day's

events. It hardly seemed possible that just twenty-four hours ago, life had seemed perfect, peaceful, normal.

Now…Brie blew out a breath and continued rocking, watching Tommy. Now she wondered if life would ever feel normal, peaceful or perfect again.

Patrick Sullivan had walked out of her shop just a few short hours ago after tossing her world upside down. She'd asked him to give her a few hours to digest the situation, and he'd agreed, with a promise that he would be back.

It had sounded like a promise, but she feared it was a threat.

After he'd left, she'd done something she'd never done before. She'd closed the shop early and hurried upstairs to her apartment, wanting nothing more than to hold Tommy in her arms, to assure herself that he was safe.

Once upstairs, she'd received another shock. She'd had a letter waiting for her in the day's mail. Or rather two. A letter from Barbara Keats's attorney advising her about Patrick Sullivan's role in her child's life, as well as a lovely lavender envelope that was too heartbreakingly familiar. It was a letter from Barbara Keats, very similar to the one she'd sent to Patrick, informing her that Patrick Sullivan was indeed Tommy's biological father.

Barbara had simply been clearing her conscience, Brie had thought with a hint of resentment. Seeing Barbara's confession written in her own hand only made the situation seem all the more real.

Panicked, Brie had placed a quick call to her attorney, the one who had handled Tommy's adoption, only to learn he was on vacation.

But she didn't need to speak to him to know the truth. Some natural instinct had told her Patrick Sullivan was indeed Tommy's father. While her heart had wanted to deny it, her mind couldn't. The evidence was far too overwhelming, from the beautiful blue of her son's eyes, to the charming dimple in his chubby cheek, to the sleek cap of ebony hair atop his head.

He was the mirror image of his father.

His father.

Another fission of fear raced over Brie, and she shivered, holding the baby closer, rocking the sleepy little boy gently in her arms.

A log shifted in the fireplace, sending up a spray of orange sparks that drifted upward into wisps of smoke. Watching the fire, Brie continued to rock, trying not to look at the clock on the mantel.

Patrick Sullivan had told her he would return. That he would not go another day, another moment without knowing, seeing, enjoying his son.

He'd meant it.

If she hadn't believed it, his phone call less than an hour ago had confirmed it. He was on his way over. She'd been tempted to grab Tommy and flee into the night. But where would she go? A woman alone with a small baby. She might be many things, but irresponsible was not one of them.

Not where her son's welfare was concerned.

She was also not cruel or selfish, and to run with Tommy would be both, not just to Patrick but to her son as well. And she couldn't deny her son his father.

She had to do what was best for her child; she had to put his needs first. And whether she liked it or not, a child needed his father.

With a sigh, Brie leaned her head back and closed her eyes, trying to ease the painful pounding in her head.

"Is he out then?" Fiona asked softly, coming into the room.

"Aye, like a light."

"It takes a lot of energy to wear out Grandma Grouch," Fiona said with an affectionate smile.

Brie frowned as Fiona reached for her coat. "And where are you going on a night like this?" Keeping her voice soft so as not to wake the baby, Brie glanced toward the window. "It looks like a storm is brewing. The sky is dark and angry. Rain seems threatening."

Fiona's gaze followed Brie's as she pulled on a rain hat, tying it securely under her chin. "A good, soft mist never hurt anyone," the older woman said, crossing the room to touch the imp's forehead. "I've a need for some fresh air."

Brie arched a brow. "And does your need for a walk have anything to do with the fact that Patrick Sullivan is coming here?"

She'd immediately told Fiona exactly what had happened with Patrick. She kept no secrets from the woman. Fiona knew her too well, just as she had known without being told that Brie's marriage to Dennis had gone horribly, terribly wrong.

In spite of her familial ties to Dennis, Fiona had quietly and steadfastly supported Brie every step of the way, from adopting Tommy, to opening the shop, and her love and loyalty to the older woman was total and encompassing.

"I've just a need for a walk," Fiona protested softly, shaking her white head. And to take care of some family business, she thought fiercely. She was going to do some inquiring around the neighborhood to see what this Sullivan clan was about. Perhaps she would even speak to the head of their clan, to warn that she would protect her own.

She was the last of the McGees, and it was her duty to see to the welfare of her kin. And see to their welfare she would. It had nearly killed her to have to quietly watch her own grandson break Brie's heart. Aye, she'd not stand by and let another man hurt Brie. Or the little imp. Nay, not while there was a breath left in her body, but there was no need to tell Brie her plans, she thought. The lass had more than enough to worry about at the moment.

"You'll be careful, then?" Brie asked worriedly, watching as Fiona went to the front closet for an umbrella.

"As always," Fiona assured her. Seeing the frown on Brie's face, Fiona crossed the room again, laying a gentle hand on Brie's shoulder. "You've enough to worry about this night, lass, don't borrow more trouble."

Patting Fiona's hand affectionately, Brie nodded, still worried. "Mind your step, then."

"As always, lass." Going to the hall closet, Fiona took out a large, black umbrella just as a gentle knock sounded at the door. Fiona turned to look at Brie, a question in her eyes.

"Will you let him in?" Brie asked softly, taking a deep breath, and hoping she was prepared for her next face to face meeting with Patrick.

Just the thought of being alone with Patrick was enough to send her pulse scampering, and she was tempted to ask Fiona to stay. She feared him, as well as her own wayward thoughts and emotions when he was around.

"Hi, Fiona." Smiling, Patrick stepped into the room, and seemed to bring a rush of energy with him. The rocker slowed as Brie's gaze took him in quickly, her eyes seeking, searching for some flaw. She found none. Although he still wore his leather jacket, unzipped and open, he'd changed into freshly pressed jeans and an ivory fisherman's knit turtleneck.

Patrick Sullivan was a beautiful man to look at, Brie decided, and she had a sneaky feeling he was a beautiful man inside, the kind a scarred, wary woman would find pleasing and comforting.

The thought scared the daylights out of her.

"Evening, Detective." Holding out a hand, Fiona waited while he took off his black leather jacket, as well as his holstered gun, then hung them both in the closet. "I'll be off now," Fiona said, glancing at Brie pointedly.

Patrick frowned. "It's starting to rain, Fiona." He glanced toward the window. "Would you like me to drive you somewhere? I'll be happy to—"

"Nay, lad. I've no need to ride. My feet are working just fine." Charmed, pleased, Fiona chuckled, reaching up to pat his cheek before she turned to Brie. "I'm off now. Kiss the little imp good night for me." She slipped out the door, shutting it quietly behind her.

Patrick stood where he was, watching Brie rock his child in her arms. It was a sight that rendered him weak and nearly speechless. Bathed in the muted golden glow of the firelight, she looked like an angel, he thought suddenly, stunned anew at the impact she had on him.

Sabrina McGee was a mystery to him, and yet, instinctively he knew that on some intimate level, he knew her, yet he had no idea *how* he knew her.

The feeling wasn't something he expected anyone to understand, because he didn't understand it. Not yet.

Still staring at her, so many thoughts, images flooded his mind. He remembered seeing a painting of the Madonna with Child, remembered how he'd felt awed by the pure beauty of the image.

The sight of Brie, rocking his child, crooning softly to Tommy, awed him now. He looked at her reverently. Golden lights haloed around her hair, turning it into a beautiful fiery mass that cascaded around her face, only emphasizing her beautiful blue eyes.

The braid was gone; she'd brushed her hair free and now it hung loose, curling around her face, cascading nearly to her elbows. He'd bet money that when she stood, it would reach her waist. He thought of that silky fiery hair spread out on a pillow. The thought came unbidden, jolting him. His fingers itched to sift through the silky strands, to feel it slide sensuously across his body, teasing, tormenting him. He suddenly ached, not his heart this time, but other, more tangible parts of his body. Ached in a way that made him want to drown himself in her, to bury himself deep inside until the ache was gone and the need sated.

"Patrick," Brie finally said, wanting only to break the unnerving silence. He was just standing there...staring at her in a way that made her stomach clench and her nerves tingle.

"Brie." He had to swallow hard to find his voice, cursing himself for letting his imagination get away from him. He couldn't afford to be having these kinds of feelings for this woman. Couldn't afford to let down his guard, not with this woman, not with any woman, especially when it came to his son.

"Please, come in."

Slowly, never taking his eyes from hers, Patrick crossed the room, coming to stand directly in front of her. The air seemed to crackle with an inexplicable, invisible tension. It was as if time had been stopped, then frozen.

Slowly Brie tilted her head to look at him, knowing immediately it was a mistake. Their gazes met, caught, held. Once again she seemed to have difficulty breathing. It had something to do with looking into his eyes. She realized that now. There was something there, something strong and far too powerful to resist. His eyes were both glorious and sad. Haunting, and yet beautiful. The kind of beauty that caused a melancholy ache of yearning. For what, she wasn't quite certain. She couldn't quite seem to put a name to it.

Patrick shifted his weight as they eyed each other warily,

the way a prizefighter might eye an opponent he wasn't quite sure of.

Finally, flustered more than she could bear, Brie dragged her gaze away to look at the baby sleeping soundly in her arms. She was finally able to take a deep relieved breath.

"He's sleeping," Patrick said softly. His eyes changed, softened, and Brie realized she would have to be blind not to see the greedy look of longing in his eyes.

It almost brought on another bout of tears. She recognized the look, for she'd worn the same look for many years—many *barren* years—every time she saw a mother and baby, and knew, for her, it was never to be.

It weakened her resolve, and she found herself flooded with compassion for Patrick. He had not asked to be robbed of his son, and had played no part in the deception. Like her, he'd been an innocent victim, so how could she resent or deny him what she herself needed for so many years?

For her, family and the need for a child had always been so basic, so necessary, she'd never questioned it. Obviously the need was just as basic and necessary for Patrick.

Somehow the thought warmed her. He was obviously a man of deep loyalty. Why else would he be here, insisting on a relationship with his son?

He was Tommy's father, and as such, was entitled to some privileges, she conceded.

So how could she selfishly deny him the right to know and love his son? Especially given the letter she'd received from her son's biological mother?

She couldn't, she realized. She simply couldn't. Her heart wouldn't allow it. Not just for Patrick's sake, but more important, for Tommy's. He needed a father. No, he needed *his* father, she realized sadly, and she simply had to get used to the idea.

What other choice did she have? Patrick had already told

her he'd resort to the court system. The thought of facing a legal battle over Tommy terrified her.

She could lose.

She wouldn't take the chance. She couldn't risk it, nor would she put Tommy through a long drawn-out legal battle. It wouldn't be fair.

She realized she had no other option. She'd invite Patrick to participate in Tommy's life, and hope and pray it was enough for him. It was perhaps the safest choice.

Brie took a slow, deep breath, her decision coming quickly. She would grant Patrick his wish, and allow him into her son's life, but she would simply guard her own heart against him. She could invite him into Tommy's life, without inviting him into her heart.

Nay, she'd be no fool over a man again. Not even one who looked as glorious as Patrick Sullivan.

Resolutely Brie took a slow, relieved breath for the first time that day.

A gentle smile filled Patrick's face, as he reached down to touch Tommy's little fist, which was still clutching Brie's blouse.

"He snores," he whispered, his smile shifting into a wide grin, amazed anew at how soft the child was.

Brie laughed softly. "Like a freight train."

"No, like Da," Patrick said softly, still stroking the baby's hand.

"Da?" Brie frowned. "Your father?"

Patrick froze for an instant, then he shook his head. "No, my grandfather." His voice was a husky whisper, creating even more intimacy between them.

"He needs to have his adenoids and tonsils out," Brie explained. "Which is why he snores. The poor little thing is also plagued by strep throat and tonsillitis in the winter, but the doctor wants to wait until he's a wee bit older."

"Surgery?" Fear ran through Patrick. He was absolutely certain he didn't like the idea of someone cutting into his son. The urge to protect his own overwhelmed him once again, and panic caused his throat to constrict. Tommy looked so small, so impossibly vulnerable.

"Hopefully we'll be able to hold off for another year or two," Brie said.

"He's...beautiful," he whispered reverently, brushing his hand against Tommy's gleaming black hair. "Just... beautiful."

Touched by the emotion in his voice, Brie looked up at him, her eyes soft, her heart momentarily unguarded.

Patrick's gaze found hers and lingered for a moment, causing a shiver to race over her.

"Aye," Brie agreed softly, her gaze never leaving his. "Like his father."

Her words surprised Patrick and he chuckled as she blushed, realizing what she'd said. He laughed again. "I don't think anyone but my mother has ever called me beautiful."

"All mothers think their babes are beautiful." She managed a grin in spite of her embarrassment. "Even if they're not." Flustered, she glanced away for a moment. "I was just going to put him down for the night, but perhaps you'd like to hold him for a moment?"

It was a small gesture that cost her nothing, but from the joy that lit Patrick's face, she realized, small or not, the gesture was one Patrick had missed and now appreciated. It gave her a small thrill of delight to know that one simple gesture of kindness had pleased him so.

She started to get up, with Tommy in her arms. Patrick reached for her arm to help her. The touch of those slender, graceful fingers, the warmth of his hand, sent nerves flood-

ing through her. She almost sat right back down, and would
have, if he hadn't had such a good grip on her arm.

"Careful." He was holding both of her elbows now,
drawing her closer to him, close enough for her to feel the
heat of his big body radiate toward her, tempting her closer.
He was close enough for her to smell the intoxicatingly
masculine scent that was distinctively his. He smelled
purely male, a scent so powerful and arousing that it
seemed to scramble her brain and her senses.

She wanted to jump back, away from him, to put some
much needed space between them, but she couldn't. Didn't.
She'd not appear foolish to him, nor would she allow herself to reveal just how he affected her.

Still holding her arms gently, Patrick tried to ignore the
fact that Brie was mere inches away from him. If he leaned
forward just a bit, he would be able to press his lips to the
top of her head, the way he longed to do this afternoon.
The way he longed to do now. But he didn't want to stop
at the top of her head; he wanted to trail his lips along a
sensuous path from the top of her head to the tips of her
toes, savoring every silky, scented inch in between.

But he didn't. Couldn't. He couldn't be a fool over another woman ever again.

He slid his hands from her arms, then held them out for
the baby. Brie transferred the sleeping bundle from her
arms to his, smiling as Tommy snuggled closer to Patrick's
warmth.

The baby's eyes fluttered open once, twice, then as if
recognizing Patrick, a blissful smile of peace slid over his
face, and Tommy snuggled deeper into slumber, reaching
out a chubby hand to grasp Patrick's sweater.

Awed, Patrick stared at the baby as Brie stared at him.
He bent his head and brushed his lips across Tommy's forehead. It was damp with sweat and made him smile.

"He smells so good." Inhaling deeply, Patrick watched his son, knowing this moment would forever be etched in the memories of his heart.

"Baby powder," Brie admitted. "I sprinkle it on his bottom after his bath each evening." When he looked at her in confusion, she explained. "To prevent diaper rash." A bit rattled that he was still standing so close, she pushed a tumble of hair off her face. "He's not quite ready to tackle the potty chair yet, but his doctor says there's no rush. As long as he's trained by the time he starts driving, it's not a problem."

Patrick's gaze flew to hers. "Driving?" he repeated in alarm, making her laugh. She laid a gentle hand on his arm.

"It was a joke," she admitted, watching the discomfort ease from his face. She shrugged. "It just means that I'm not to rush him. When he's ready, he'll let me know."

"I see." He wasn't sure he saw anything of the kind. Each tiny bit of information about his son, every piece of knowledge, he carefully committed to memory, storing the information for future use.

"Would you like to see his room?" Sensing his need to know about his son, Brie felt generous enough to want to share these harmless bits of Tommy's life with him.

"I'd love to." Carrying Tommy, he followed Brie out of the living room and down the long hallway to the baby's room. He couldn't help but grin as he glanced around. Obviously Brie's talent for decorating started in her son's room. It looked like a room out of a child's fairy tale. Everywhere he looked there were bright colors destined to catch a child's eye. And imagination. This was a room where a boy's dreams were made.

The walls were papered in "Sesame Street" characters, and a large shelf ran along the entire perimeter. Atop it sat various characters from the popular television show, posed in various positions as if they were having a friendly conversation.

The entire room was a magical, mystical playland meant for sweet dreaming. What a wonderful place for a child to grow up, he thought with a smile. Frowning suddenly, he wondered why the crib was set smack-dab in the middle of the room.

Watching him, Brie saw his confusion, tugged his sleeve and whispered, "I have to move the crib into the middle of the room at night, because in the morning when he wakes, he has a tendency to be very hungry and very impatient. He takes his empty bottle or his toys and pounds on the wall with them to get my attention." She grinned. "I've had to repaper that wall twice now."

She moved to the crib, taking Tommy from his arms and laying him gently down. Instinctively she reached down to cover Tommy. He gave a loud snore, rolled over and snuggled into a ball, tangling the blanket between his legs and feet.

Habit had Brie reaching for the battered, furry green Oscar the Grouch stuffed animal sitting in the corner of the crib. She tucked it under the baby's arm.

"If he wakes and Oscar's not there, he cries." She stood over her son for a moment, her heart filled with love. She glanced at Patrick, saw the loving expression on his face, and knew immediately that her decision to let him share in Tommy's life was the right one.

For Tommy's sake.

Brie touched his arm gently, and Patrick turned to follow her out of the room. He paused suddenly, his gaze lingering on his sleeping son, wanting to absorb every precious moment he could, to make up for all the moments he'd lost.

He wasn't certain what he'd expected when he'd returned here, wasn't certain what Brie's reaction would be, but he was pleased that some of the fear and resentment seemed to have left her. He felt grateful that she'd given him this…this little peek into her son's life, his routine. It made him feel so much more a part of Tommy's life.

But it wasn't enough, he thought firmly, turning toward Brie and following her out of the room and back down the hall. It wasn't nearly enough.

But how was he going to make her understand that he wanted more, so much more?

Aware that Patrick was right behind her, and without Tommy as a barrier between them, Brie suddenly felt nervous. Wiping her damp palms down her thighs, she forced a smile as she turned to him.

"Would you like some coffee?" She'd stick to the mundane, and hope that it would help her nerves. Keeping busy would calm her hands if nothing else. "I made a fresh pot just a little bit ago."

Patrick came to a halt at the entrance to the living room. He hadn't paid that much attention when he'd arrived, but now he glanced around, smiling at the comfortable, homey feel of her apartment. Because it was above her store, he had expected it to be small, cramped and perhaps a bit impersonal. It was anything but.

The rooms were large, at least the living room he was standing in was, and it was gorgeous. It was an old building, with large airy rooms with high ceilings and almost floor-to-ceiling windows. A fire was roaring in the huge stone fireplace that took up one wall, while the other three walls were filled with bookcases filled with row after row of what looked like much loved, much read books. The floors were a planked oak, with a couple Oriental carpets thrown about. The carpets picked up the coloring of the room which was done in various shades of blue and white.

A clear glass fluted lamp with a scalloped navy shade sat in a corner and cast a warm glow over the room.

There was a large, overstuffed navy-and-white-print sofa with a matching love seat. The connected dining room had a large oak trestle table, with navy leather Queen Anne chairs at each end, and four oak ladder-back chairs along the sides. A large elegantly framed Monet print in various shades of blue took up nearly one wall in the dining room, the colors picking up the hue of the wallpaper.

Right smack-dab in front of the fireplace stood the rocker where Brie had been sitting with Tommy when he'd first arrived.

There was something so warm, so homey about the place, and then he realized it was because it reminded him so much of *his* home. The one he'd grown up in, surrounded by his brothers, his mother, Da, Katie. Surrounded by love.

"Your home is lovely."

Pleased at his compliment, she smiled, dipping her hands in the pockets of her slacks so he wouldn't see them trembling.

"Thank you."

He followed her into the kitchen, which was just as large and spacious as the rest of the apartment. But unlike the rest of the elegant old apartment, it had been updated and modernized, and now boasted state-of-the-art appliances, as well as a new ceramic floor in varying shades of blue and white in keeping with the overall color scheme.

As Brie retrieved a cup from the cabinet, and poured him some coffee, Patrick's eyes were drawn to the sparkling white refrigerator where an assortment of pictures obviously scribbled and colored by a child were hanging.

They brought an ache to his heart. He'd missed so much of his son's life—hours, days and months that he'd never be able to recapture. He'd never realized how precious time was until now.

He loved his child so.

"Those are Tommy's," she said softly, glancing at the pictures as she handed him his coffee. "I enrolled him in a twice-a-week play group for two-year-olds. Since he's an only child, with just Fiona and I for company, I thought it was important for him to have other children to play with, so that he learned to share and get along with others."

Patrick turned to her and Brie averted her gaze, stunned anew by the impact those blue eyes had on her.

"He loves it," she added, suddenly feeling foolish and tongue-tied and not knowing why. Patrick Sullivan was indeed a fine-looking man and was having a strange effect on her. She simply had to remember that she'd resolved to let him into her son's life, not into her heart.

Brie suddenly laughed. "There's a cute little blonde in Tommy's play group, an older woman, almost three, that I think he has a particular fondness for."

"Ahh." Pleased, Patrick nodded. "An older woman, huh?" He shook his head. "He already has a way with the ladies. Now I know for sure he's a Sullivan." Immediately he regretted his words at the look on her face. "I'm sorry, Brie. I didn't mean...I meant that as a joke." Shifting his weight, he sipped his coffee, cursing his careless tongue.

"It's all right, Patrick." She let out a breath and turned to reach for her own coffee. "I'll just have to get used to it." And him. She was no longer accustomed to having a man underfoot, in her house or her kitchen. It was going to take some getting used to, she realized, hoping she could control her own feelings and remember her resolve so she didn't make a complete donkey out of herself.

Patrick touched her shoulders, gently turning her toward him again, pained by the look in her eyes, her face. He left his hands resting on her shoulders, remembering how slender, how delicate she was from when he'd held her in his arms.

"Brie, I know this has been…difficult for you, but I want to thank you, for giving me this." His gaze, serious and solemn, searched hers. He hesitated for a moment, trying to put his feelings into words. "I have such a need to know about him. Everything. Every little detail. When he took his first step. His first word. His favorite food. There's so many things I don't know, yet need to know."

She let out a breath that seemed too heavy to hold in any longer. "I know. I understand. I truly do." She shook her head, wishing his hands weren't so warm as they rested atop her shoulders. "I'm trying," she explained with a shrug. "But it might take me a while."

"I understand, Brie." He waited until she lifted her gaze to his, and the haunted look in her eyes had his guts clenching. He wanted nothing more than to soothe that look away. She pulled at him in places that he never wanted to be off balance again, not to a woman. But she made him feel off balance with those eyes, that smile, that face. With some effort, he tried to harden his heart.

"All I want is the opportunity to get to know my son, to be part of his life so that he knows he does indeed have a father, one who loves him and will always be there for him. He needs and deserves a father. Every little boy does."

"Aye, I know," she whispered, wishing he wasn't standing quite so close and his words weren't tugging quite so hard at her heart. The kitchen suddenly felt small, cramped and airless.

"I know what it's like to grow up without a father, Brie, and I don't want that for Tommy."

His words reminded her of something, and she looked

up at him curiously. "You lost your father." It wasn't a question, but a statement as her gaze searched his.

Slowly he nodded, feeling something tighten in his throat. Patrick hadn't spoken about his father since the day he'd been prematurely killed in the line of duty.

"My father...was a police officer, just like his father." Taking a deep breath, Patrick wondered why he was telling her this. "It's a Sullivan family tradition to enter the force," he said with a shrug. "My father was killed in the line of duty when I was barely eight years old." He shook his head. "I don't think I ever got over it."

"Oh, Patrick." The need to offer comfort was instinctive. Brie didn't think, she merely reacted, lifting a hand to his cheek. "I'm so sorry."

Her heart went out to him. The man had lost his father, and then his son. He had a right to be hurt, to be angry, to feel resentment. Now she understood some of his determination to be part of Tommy's life. Clearly, he didn't want his own son to face the same fate. Now she understood him so much better.

"I was fortunate enough to have my own father until shortly before my marriage," she said. "It was a blessing I've been grateful for every single day." Those gorgeous eyes of his were sad, yet filled with understanding and such unbearable bleakness she found herself wanting to ease his desolation. "Tommy is a lucky lad to have a father who loves and wants him. And who wants to be part of his life." As she said the words, she knew that, in spite of her own fears, they were the truth.

For the first time since Patrick Sullivan had walked into her life and turned it upside down, she felt a bout of gratitude for his presence. It would be to Tommy's benefit, she reasoned.

"Brie." Touched by her concern, Patrick pressed her

hand to his mouth for a kiss. She tasted as sweet as he'd expected. He watched her eyes widen, her lashes flutter with nervousness, and kissed her hand again.

Rattled, Brie slowly withdrew her hand, unwilling to allow herself to be charmed by this man. He held the power of her world in his hand, the power to take Tommy from her. She could never relax or let down her guard around him knowing what was at stake.

Nervous now, and not wanting to be the sole focus of his attention, Brie set her coffee cup down, then slipped free of him and went to the refrigerator. She selected a picture, one brightly colored and gaily scribbled. One corner was curled, there was a sticky little hand print in another, and the bottom was a bit ragged, as if Tommy had thought it a snack. Brie ran her hand gently over the paper.

"I think...I think...Tommy would like it if you had this." She handed the picture to him, grateful she was able to relinquish this small part of her child with grace. It didn't hurt nearly as much as she thought, perhaps because she felt Patrick's feelings were genuine. But she knew her trust would be slow in coming.

Touched beyond measure, Patrick took the picture, handling it as if it were the most fragile, precious gem.

"Thank you," he said softly, his gaze going over every inch of it. He looked at her, then stroked a hand down her cheek. "It was a lovely, generous gesture."

She took a deep breath. It was time to get down to the practicalities. "I think we need to discuss how we're going to handle this situation."

Patrick nodded.

"Why don't we take our coffee into the living room in front of the fire?" She ran her hands up and down her arms, chilled. "I thought you might like to see all the scrapbooks I've kept of Tommy since his birth." She smiled at the pleasure that lit his face. He looked like a little boy at Christmas. Perhaps it wouldn't be so hard to share, at least not her memories. It was a little thing, and certainly a good-will gesture.

"I'd love to."

Grabbing their cups, Brie refilled them, then carried them into the living room. The fire was burning low, so she set the cups down, removed the safety screen, then fed more wood into the flames. The fire hissed, shifted, then sent up a large flame, making her smile.

Patrick began to relax, and settled himself comfortably on the couch. Obviously his son was in good, caring hands.

"Shouldn't Fiona be back by now?" Patrick asked as he glanced out the window. The darkness had grown deeper, the wind stronger.

Brie glanced out the window with a frown, realizing just how late it was getting. "Probably." Her frown deepened as her gaze shifted to the large clock on the fireplace. "She's been gone a long time. I'm afraid I'm a bit worried. It's not like her to just take off like this." She pressed her nose against the window. "At least the rain's finally stopped." She rubbed her chilled arms again. She always got cold when she was nervous. And Patrick Sullivan made her nervous with his size and his presence, as well as his intentions.

Worried now himself, Patrick sat forward. "Do you want me to go out and look for her, Brie? Or I could call the station and have one of the patrols look for her."

Brie couldn't help it, she started to laugh, touched in spite of herself at his kindness and concern. "Thank you, Patrick, for your kind and generous offer, but I'm afraid if I sent a police patrol searching for Fiona, I'd not hear the end of it. Ever." Her lips settled into a grin. "She may be up in age, but she's still a stubborn, prideful woman, and she'd consider it an insult that I'd doubted her ability to look after herself." Still, Brie continued to gaze out into the dark night, concern etched in her brow. "I wonder where she's gone," she wondered aloud. "And what she's up to," she added worriedly.

Sullivan's Pub had sat on the same corner in Logan Square for over fifty years. Located a few blocks from the Fourteenth District Police Station, and right under the elevated tracks, it had been a cop's hangout and the Sullivan family's enterprise since the day it had opened.

Generally filled with raucous police officers and neighborhood regulars, as well as any number of members of the growing Sullivan clan, at this hour on a chilly Monday evening, the bar was virtually empty.

From his ever-present spot behind the bar, Da casually glanced up when the door opened, bringing a chill into the spacious room.

He'd been wiping down a few imaginary spots on the scarred wooden bar, but his hand stilled and he merely stared at the woman framed in the doorway, closing an umbrella, a rain bonnet tied securely under her chin.

He looked at her curiously. His eyes saw a woman of about his age, with snow-white hair and stormy blue eyes, but his heart saw a beautiful young lass with sparkling blue eyes and an engaging smile. A woman of spirit and determination, he decided immediately. And if he was reading her right, temper as well. It tickled him and he felt a grin sneak up on him wondering who she was and what she was about. He had a feeling it was going to be interesting to find out.

He watched her march toward him, chin lifted, eyes flashing, umbrella and pocketbook clutched to her side as if she had the Queen's wealth contained in it.

Without removing his gaze from hers, he slowly began wiping the bar down again, trying to disguise the feelings that were making his heart thud and his palms damp.

"Are you of the Sullivan clan?" she asked, and his grin widened as he heard the familiar lilting tones of his homeland.

"Aye." He nodded. "I am, indeed. Sean Patrick Sullivan," he said, extending his hand in welcome to her. "Head of the clan."

A bit startled by the familiar sound of her homeland, Fiona stared at the man's big beefy hand for a moment before taking it. His hand was rough, callused, yet warm with life.

"Fiona McGee," she said with a nod of her own, trying to ignore the immediate impact he'd had on her. "And we've business to discuss, Sean Patrick Sullivan." Eyes glinting in determination, her chin lifted. "*Clan* business."

Chapter Five

"**Y**ou're very close to Fiona, aren't you?" Patrick asked as she continued to stare out the window.

Brie nodded, turning back to him. "She's the only family I have left now." She shrugged. "It's just Fiona, Tommy and me. We're our own little family."

"Well, Brie, I'd like to be part of your little family. If you let me." Patrick held out his hand.

She looked at his hand for a long moment, feeling terribly off center and just a bit frightened. Until now, Tommy had been hers. *She* had been all the family he needed.

Remembering she'd been given no choice in the matter, she swallowed the ball of resentment that bubbled at his words.

She merely stared at his hand as if it were a serpent ready to strike. She was being ridiculous, she told herself. Absolutely, utterly ridiculous. It was merely a friendly gesture, yet Brie knew instinctively, automatically, how her body would react if she took his hand, if she touched him. She might be trying to forget what his touch had done to her, but her body hadn't, and she couldn't risk it. She'd not allow her emotions to get entangled with this man.

She couldn't think about him as a man, or how unaccountably aware he made her feel as a woman. It was too much for her to handle right now. All of it. His real identity, his wanting to be part of Tommy's life, her own reluctant feelings for him. She was going to have to compartmentalize the situation in order to keep her wits about her.

It shouldn't be hard. She was a businesswoman, and knew full well the benefits of prioritizing and compartmentalizing.

Now, she just had to keep Patrick in his own little compartment, which had nothing to do with her on a personal level, as a woman, and she'd be fine.

Smiling to disguise her fear, Brie ignored his question and his outstretched hand and went to the hutch in the dining room and extracted several bound scrapbooks, which she'd promised to show Patrick.

"I started these when Tommy was first born." She smiled, running her hand lovingly over the smooth leather. "I didn't want to forget anything, and so I started saving things. Little bits and pieces from his life so that when he was grown, I could show them to him." She glanced down at the book. On the cover was Tommy's birth announcement with a picture of him when he was just a few days old. "I thought you might like to see them." Crossing the room, she sat down on the couch next to Patrick, close enough to share the book, yet not quite close enough to touch. She was still feeling unsettled by the memory of his soft lips on her hand.

Draping his arm along the back of the couch, Patrick eyed the book with interest.

"This was the first picture taken of him. In the hospital," she explained, glancing up at Patrick, vividly aware of how close he was to her. His face, his mouth was just...inches away from hers. She swallowed hard. "As you can see, he had a full head of black hair even at birth."

Something strange crawled over Patrick as he looked at his son as a newborn. "He looks just like a Sullivan." He glanced at Brie. Something was nagging at him, and he sensed this might be the time to satisfy his curiosity. "Brie, why did you adopt Tommy?"

She stilled for a moment. Taking a deep breath, she turned to him. "Why?" She shook her head as if she didn't understand the question. "What do you mean, why?"

"I mean, why did you decide to adopt?" He watched her carefully, noted the stiffening of her shoulders, the way her gaze averted his. Without thought he laid a hand over hers. "I'm sorry, I didn't mean to pry or get personal. I was just...curious."

She nodded, trying to ignore the skidding of her pulse and the warmth of his touch.

"It's...all right," she conceded, realizing it was a fair question and deserved an answer. Hesitantly she lifted her gaze to his. "I found out shortly after I married that I couldn't...have children." Her voice was so soft and so wounded, Patrick instinctively tightened his hand over hers.

Taking a deep breath, she continued. "But I'd always wanted children." She smiled. "Lots and lots of them. But unfortunately it wasn't to be." She shrugged her slender shoulders. "So adoption seemed the only alternative."

His gaze searched hers. There was something else there, something she wasn't telling him. "And how did your...husband feel about adopting?" he asked hesitantly. He hated to admit he was curious about the man who had shared her life and her bed.

Self-conscious now, and deathly ashamed to admit the

PLAY TIC-TAC-TOE

OR FREE BOOKS AND A GREAT FREE GIFT!

Use this sticker to **PLAY TIC-TAC-TOE.** See instructions inside!

THERE'S NO COST∗NO OBLIGATION!

Get **2** books and a fabulous mystery gift! **ABSOLUTELY FREE!**

Turn the page to play!

Play TIC-TAC-TOE and get FREE GIFTS!

HOW TO PLAY:

1. Play the tic-tac-toe scratch-off game at the right for your FREE BOOKS and FREE GIFT!

2. Send back this card and you'll receive TWO brand-new Silhouette Romance® novels. These books have a cover price of $3.50 each, but they are yours to keep absolutely free.

3. There's no catch. You're under no obligation to buy anything. We charge nothing — ZERO — for your first shipment. And you don't have to make any minimum number of purchases — not even one!

4. The fact is, thousands of readers enjoy receiving books by mail from the Silhouette Reader Service™ months before they're available in stores. They like the convenience of home delivery, and they love our discount prices!

5. We hope that after receiving your free books you'll want to remain a subscriber. But the choice is yours — to continue or cancel, any time at all! So why not take us up on our invitation, with no risk of any kind. You'll be glad you did!

YOURS FREE A FABULOUS MYSTERY GIFT!

We can't tell you what it is... but we're sure you'll like it!

A FREE GIFT — just for playing

TIC-TAC-TOE!

First, scratch the gold boxes on the tic-tac-toe board. Then remove the "X" sticker from the front and affix it so that you get three X's in a row. This means you can get TWO FREE Silhouette Romance® novels and a **FREE MYSTERY GIFT!**

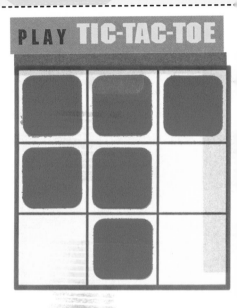

PLAY TIC-TAC-TOE

YES! Please send me all the gifts for which I qualify. I understand that I am under no obligation to purchase any books, as explained on the back of this card.

(U-SIL-R-08/98)

215 SDL CH6S

Name

(PLEASE PRINT CLEARLY)

Address _____ Apt.#

City _____ State _____ Zip

Offer limited to one per household and not valid to current Silhouette Romance® subscribers. All orders subject to approval.
© 1997 HARLEQUIN ENTERPRISES LTD.
® and TM are trademarks owned by
Harlequin Books S.A., used under license.

PRINTED IN U.S.A.

DETACH AND MAIL CARD TODAY!

The Silhouette Reader Service™ — Here's how it works:

Accepting free books places you under no obligation to buy anything. You may keep the books and gift and return the shipping statement marked "cancel." If you do not cancel, about a month later we'll send you 6 additional novels and bill you just $2.90 each, plus 25¢ delivery per book and applicable sales tax, if any.*
That's the complete price — and compared to cover prices of $3.50 each — quite a bargain! You may cancel at any time, but if you choose to continue, every month we'll send you 6 more books, which you may either purchase at the discount price...or return to us and cancel your subscription.

*Terms and prices subject to change without notice. Sales tax applicable in N.Y.

If offer card is missing write to: Silhouette Reader Service, 3010 Walden Ave., P.O. Box 1867, Buffalo NY 14240-1867

BUSINESS REPLY MAIL

FIRST-CLASS MAIL   PERMIT NO. 717   BUFFALO, NY

POSTAGE WILL BE PAID BY ADDRESSEE

SILHOUETTE READER SERVICE
3010 WALDEN AVE
PO BOX 1867
BUFFALO NY 14240-9952

NO POSTAGE
NECESSARY
IF MAILED
IN THE
UNITED STATES

truth, Brie struggled to pull her hand free of his, but he held on tight.

"Brie?" His voice, gentle and soft, prodded her. She didn't want to answer him; didn't want to have to admit the truth. But she had no choice. She had a feeling he would keep prying until she told him what he wanted to know.

"Dennis...Dennis was of the old school," she began by way of explanation. "He agreed to adopt at first because he knew how much a child meant to me."

"At first?" Alarm bells began going off in Patrick's mind. "What do you mean?"

Needing something to do with her hands, she slipped free of him and clutched the scrapbook like a lifeline. "I wanted a child so...desperately, and when I learned of Tommy's imminent birth, it seemed as if at least some of my prayers had been answered." Her voice had dropped to a whisper that echoed softly around the quiet room. "We had registered with a private attorney. Dennis had agreed to it, but I'm sure he thought nothing would ever come of it. When the lawyer contacted us to tell us there was a baby available if we wanted him, Dennis made it clear he really wasn't interested in raising a child that wasn't his own." She was struggling with the tears that she'd held in far too long. "He never thought anything would come of our adoption request."

"He didn't want Tommy." The knowledge seemed to cut somewhere deep in Patrick's heart, and he dropped an arm to her shoulder to draw her close, wanting to give comfort as much as get it. This was his child they were talking about.

His child.

And hers.

Her words angered Patrick in a way nothing had in a long, long time. He couldn't understand anyone not wanting or caring for a helpless little baby. Nor could he understand a husband emotionally abandoning his wife in that way.

It was not the way he was raised. Family was everything. And your wife, your mate, the person you were destined to be with, deserved all your love, loyalty and respect. Anything else was merely cheating yourself. And your wife.

He'd never understand that kind of man.

For a moment, Brie held herself stiffly, fighting the urge to accept his comfort. But the need was stronger than her resolve and she allowed herself to relax against him.

"Go on," he whispered. She was close enough now that he could smell her scent. It was comforting and familiar in a way that stunned him.

He felt her sigh against his chest. It was filled with silent shudders. "Dennis finally agreed to the adoption only because if he didn't, he knew..." Her voice trailed off. She didn't even want to think of that horrible, hurtful time. The cold shock of reality, of finding out that the man she thought she knew—the man she had married—had deceived her on the most basic level. He was not the man he purported to be. It was all a lie. Their marriage. His love. All lies.

It had been heartbreaking for her, realizing the truth about the man she had married. A man she had loved. But his coldness and cruelty to her, and toward Tommy, had killed any love she had for him.

She took another deep, shuddering breath in order to continue. "Dennis made it clear that Tommy was *my* son. I wanted him, so I would have to take full responsibility and raise him." She couldn't bear to look at Patrick, knowing how much he wanted her son, and knowing how much her own husband hadn't. It seemed so unfair.

"And you did?"

Surprised, she glanced at him. "But of course. Why wouldn't I?"

His arm was still around her, and his fingers toyed with the curling ends of her hair. "Because you could have changed your mind and kept peace in your marriage."

"Aye," she said slowly, turning to look at him, meeting his gaze in spite of the fact that his closeness made her heart feel as if it were trying to leap from her chest. "Perhaps I could have changed my mind," she conceded in a whisper. "But how could I have changed my heart?" The question seemed to hang in the air between them for a moment.

He shook his head, wanting nothing more than to gather her in his arms. But he resisted the urge. "You are an incredible woman, Brie." Smiling, he stroked a hand down the silk of her hair. "Absolutely incredible." She'd given up a lot to be a mother to his child. It had been a brave, courageous and totally selfless act. She'd known what she'd lose if she adopted Tommy, but she'd done it anyway.

Gratitude nearly overwhelmed him. It was almost ironic that Tommy's biological mother had given him up, while Brie had given up so much to get him.

"Nay, Patrick," she corrected. "Not incredible at all." She managed a smile. "Just a mother. From the moment I laid eyes on the little imp, I loved him as nothing else before or since."

She didn't have to tell him of her love, he could see it in her eyes, in her every gesture toward Tommy. "Dennis wasn't…abusive…?"

Alarmed by his train of thoughts, Brie's head came up and she laid a hand on his chest. His sweater was of the softest wool and warmed her cold hand. She could feel the rapid beating of his heart, and it seemed to match her own.

"No, he never hurt the boy. He wasn't a cruel man—

not in the way you think, Patrick. Just an insecure one who felt that only a child of his blood could really be his son.''

''I wasn't talking about Tommy,'' he informed her quietly. ''I have no doubt you'd never allow anything or anyone to hurt him.''

Her smile bloomed and he felt an instant sense of relief. ''Of that you can be sure,'' she said.

He had a feeling she'd protect Tommy with her life if need be. He felt his admiration for her grow. ''I was talking about how Dennis treated you.''

''Oh.'' It was all she could manage to say. She'd never discussed her disappointment with anyone. Nor the fears or the hurt that lay like cobwebs on her scarred heart.

''He hurt you.'' It was a statement of fact that needed no confirmation. She'd told him more than enough; he could surmise the rest. Perhaps that explained why she was so wary of him, that and the circumstances, of course. But he knew it had been something more than just the circumstances.

She tried to shrug away his concern. ''He's gone now, and I won't speak ill of him.'' She lifted her chin to look at Patrick, alarmed at the way her system responded every time she looked into his eyes. It was as if a flock of butterflies had taken flight in her tummy, tickling her heart.

''Dennis was, in his own way, a good man, but he never got over the fact that I couldn't give him his own sons. It shamed him that his own wife couldn't give him a namesake.''

''That's ridiculous,'' Patrick declared, furious. ''And stupidly old-fashioned. There's nothing to be ashamed about,'' he said, knowing the shame she was talking about was hers to bear. ''Nor does it justify his emotional abandonment of you.''

Abandonment. Until Patrick had said the word, she'd

never been able to verbalize the absolute desolation and fear she'd felt when her marriage had unraveled right before her eyes. Dennis had turned a cold heart to her. From the moment she'd brought Tommy home, he'd never again touched her. Not in kindness. Not in anger. Certainly not in love. The last year of their marriage had been so difficult. If she hadn't had Fiona, she had no idea what she would have done.

She took a deep breath, not wanting to discuss the matter further. "Anyway, it's done and over with now." Wanting to change the subject, Brie opened the scrapbook. "This is Tommy's birth certificate."

Peering down, Patrick frowned, wishing he'd been able to ask her more about her marriage and her husband. He had a feeling it explained why she seemed so skittish of him.

"Why on earth does it list your name and Dennis's as the birth parents?" he asked suddenly, the typed words on the document finally registering. The flare of resentment and jealousy surprised him.

"That surprised me, as well," she admitted with a small smile. "But in this state, when you legally adopt a child, you get a birth certificate showing you as the birth parents." She shrugged, not understanding all the legalities of the situation. "I guess it's because adoption records are still sealed to give the birth parents and the child privacy."

Patrick wasn't entirely certain this pleased him. Having Dennis McGee listed as Tommy's father certainly did not.

He sighed in relief. He had no desire to wish harm or ill to anyone, but he was secretly grateful that Dennis McGee would no longer have a chance to hurt either Brie or his son.

Brie turned a page in the scrapbook and started to laugh. "Fiona took this picture when I gave Tommy his first bath.

Notice most of the water is on me.'' She shook her head. ''The imp still hates to take a bath.''

''Maybe you just need some expert help,'' he quipped with a smile. He watched the challenge register in her eyes.

''Expert help, is it?'' Shaking her head, she laughed. ''I promise no matter how expert the help, you're bound to end up as wet as he.''

''I think I can handle it.'' He remembered giving his sister-in-law Joanna a hand bathing the triplets, and wondered how a woman with only two arms managed to handle three little spirited bundles. ''I have a little experience. I do have nieces and nephews.''

She nodded, wondering just how long it would be until Patrick Sullivan grew tired or bored with the mundane, everyday duties of being a parent. It wasn't all joys and laughter, but hard work and worry.

''Being a parent is not an easy job,'' she commented.

''I don't expect it to be.'' He turned to her. The glow from the fire was glinting off her hair, making it sparkle like fire. ''I'm not looking for excitement or glamour, Brie, just a chance to be a father to my son.''

''Very well.'' She nodded, since the matter apparently had been settled. ''Perhaps then, we should agree on a few things. I'm more than ready to share Tommy, to welcome you into his life, as is your right, but I think we need to agree that we will always put Tommy's wants, needs and desires above our own.''

''That goes without saying.''

''And if you decide that you'd rather not...take on the responsibility of fatherhood, you will tell me immediately.'' A shadow crossed her features. ''I don't want him hurt again. Not ever.''

The tone of her voice tore at his heart. He reached for her hand. ''I promise you here and now that I will never,

ever grow tired of being Tommy's father. This isn't a game, Brie. This is my life. He's my son.''

"Aye, but please try to remember, he's *my* son, as well.'' He saw the fear then, shadowed in her eyes, and sought to reassure her. Tugging her close, he dropped his arm around her again.

"Brie, I'll never forget that. I owe you a great debt of gratitude. You've been a wonderful mother to him, given him all the things a child needs. I promise I'll never do anything to jeopardize your relationship with Tommy. Why would I?'' He shook his head. "It would only hurt him and I wouldn't do anything to hurt that boy. Not anything.''

"Good.'' Relieved, she dared a glance at him. "But you're not to be spoiling the little imp, not that he's not spoiled enough.'' She lifted her chin higher and their eyes met, held. She felt her heart tumble over wickedly in her chest. Those eyes of his, she thought, they made her feel things, want things she knew she couldn't have or handle.

Not just because of Tommy, although that was reason enough, but because of her own fragile heart. She'd never be vulnerable to a man again, especially one who looked so good, and smelled so sinful, and had such power over her and her son. She'd learned her lesson well.

Patrick grinned a mischievous grin. "A little spoiling never hurt anyone.''

"Oh, Lord,'' she muttered. "Why do I have the feeling I'm going to have my hands full?''

He laughed and gave her a quick hug of camaraderie that surprised them both.

Immediately, Brie's eyes widened, but not before he saw the flare of desire darken them. She drew back from him, trying not to show how alarmed she was by his nearness.

Brie swallowed hard, trying to get her mind on their discussion, and not on the feelings roaring through her.

"Would you like to come to dinner tomorrow?" Clutching the scrapbooks like a lifeline, she glanced at him. "Tomorrow's Tuesday, and we usually eat as soon as the shop closes at five. Since Tommy doesn't go to his play group, he's usually wound up and a bit rambunctious. Having a new face might be just what he needs to calm him."

"I'd like that," Patrick said, pleased beyond belief.

She took a deep breath. "I think he'll need a few days to get adjusted to you, to having a new person in his life."

"I'd like to spend as much time as possible with him."

"But what about your detective work?" she asked with a frown, wanting—needing—to know just exactly how much time he planned to spend with Tommy.

And her.

Patrick stifled a yawn. "I'm on the midnight shift now, so most of my days are free."

"Midnight?" Brie's gaze went to the mantel clock. "Patrick, do you mean to tell me you have to work tonight?" She hadn't given any thought at all to his job. Here they'd been sitting, talking away the evening.

He glanced at his watch. "In about an hour." He stifled another yawn. He hadn't had much sleep since he'd received those letters, hadn't had much peace, either. But tonight, sitting in front of the fire, discussing his son, he'd been more relaxed than he'd been in days.

"Is it dangerous?" she asked quietly. "Your job?" She hadn't even considered the possibility until now. She remembered him taking off his weapon when he came in the door. It made her want to shiver.

"Dangerous?" Patrick shook his head, not wanting to worry her. "Living can be dangerous," he said lightly, tugging at the ends of her hair. He grinned. "My schedule will give me a lot of time to spend with Tommy. And you'll get a break. It probably hasn't been easy being a round-the-clock, twenty-four-hour-a-day mom, while trying to run the shop and do everything else.''

Slowly she set the scrapbooks down on the table. ''It's a labor of love, Patrick. All of it. The shop. Tommy. I never get tired of any of it.'' It was the truth, she realized. But to no one would she admit that sometimes she did wish there were more hours in the day.

The phone rang and Brie expelled a relieved breath and got up to answer it. She spoke briefly, then hung up with a smile.

''Fiona,'' she said by way of explanation as she reclaimed her seat. ''She's getting a ride home from a friend and said not to worry.''

Brie hesitated for a moment, then decided she needed to pick up the thread of their conversation. ''Patrick, it might take me some time to get used to…sharing him with you. He's been mine—just mine—for so long…'' Her voice trailed off.

''I understand.'' And he did. He reached for her hand, vowing to do nothing to hurt or threaten this woman who had given his child so much. ''I promise I'll try not to make a pest of myself, and I'll try not to disrupt your schedule too much.'' He linked his fingers through hers, amazed at how delicate she was. ''Brie, I don't know that I'll ever be able to tell you how much this means to me.''

''You don't have to,'' she said. ''I know what it's like to want a child, to feel the need inside.'' She laid her free hand on his heart, wanting him to know she understood—in her mind, at least.

It was her protective heart that was giving her problems with the situation. ''Here, where the need is the greatest. I do understand, and I promise I'll try to give you what you need.''

He kissed her hand. ''Thank you.'' There seemed to be

a moment of awkward silence, and he knew he'd unnerved her again by kissing her hand. He understood she felt frightened and threatened, but there was also something else that spooked her. What sizzled and sparked between them. The connection that seemed to be tugging them closer while their circumstances pulled them apart.

He had to remember his priorities here. And first and foremost, they included his son. He couldn't afford to have feelings on a personal level, especially for this woman. He'd been badly burned by trusting another woman where his child was concerned. He wouldn't—couldn't—do it again.

He was still holding her hand, and it seemed calm and strong and so incredibly warm.

"So then you'll come for dinner tomorrow?" she asked.

"Definitely." He stood up, taking her with him. With his free hand he reached for the picture she'd given him, the one Tommy had drawn. "And I'll even bring dessert."

She laughed. "You'd best bring a change of clothes if you plan on bathing your boy."

"My boy," he said reverently, a silly grin sliding across his features. "That sure has a nice ring to it."

Still holding his hand, she walked him to the door, releasing him to open the closet to get his coat and gun. She stared at the leather shoulder holster, and the wicked-looking weapon inside. Gingerly she ran the tip of her finger over it.

"It looks…frightening." Running her hands up her arms to ease the sudden chill and fear that gripped her, Brie tried not to think of the damage a weapon like that could inflict.

She couldn't start worrying about Patrick, she thought in annoyance, unwilling to admit that was exactly what she was doing. She had enough things on her plate to worry about now. But still, for a moment she wished that he had a nice safe job…dressing department-store dummies. For Tommy's sake, she quietly amended. She didn't want her son to find his father, only to lose him.

Aware that his gun had made her nervous, Patrick retrieved the holster and slipped it on in a gesture that was as familiar and natural to him as breathing. He'd worn it so long, it seemed like a second skin to him.

"A weapon is not dangerous if you know how to use it." It was a standard line he'd repeated often to civilians, especially to his mother, Maeve. Even after all these years, and all her experience with a family of cops, guns still made her nervous.

"Do you like…police work?" She'd never known a police officer before, at least not personally.

"I can't imagine doing anything else."

The tone of his voice had her gaze shifting from his gun to his face. She saw it then, the look of absolute, utter joy. It was the same look he had when he looked at Tommy. She realized then how complex this man was.

Patrick was thoughtful for a moment, wondering if she would be able to understand how he felt about his job, and wondering why it was important to him that she did.

"Brie, I was raised to believe that it's important to give back to the community. It's not enough to just take from life. You have to give something back, as well. Becoming a cop is not just a family tradition, but…a way of life for me and my brothers. I like the idea of being able to help people. Of knowing that they trust me to protect and defend them."

Patrick Sullivan was an unusual man, she realized, touched more than she believed possible.

"But isn't it a huge…responsibility? To have so many relying on you?"

Patrick laughed. "I never thought of it as a responsibility." He shrugged. "Actually, I think it's an honor. I would have become a cop even if it wasn't a family tradition."

She nodded. It was hard not to see the genuine goodness of this man. He wore his character on his sleeve the way others wore cuff links. She would not be charmed by it, she admonished herself, knowing it was too late.

It was hard not to compare this man's character and sense of honor and responsibility for mere strangers to the husband who hadn't even had a sense of honor for his own wife and child. The thought brought a quick pang of hurt and remorse.

"Tommy is very lucky to have such an honorable man for a father," she said slowly, making him smile.

He dropped his hands to her shoulders, wondering why that shadow of pain was in her eyes again.

"And very lucky to have such a beautiful, loving mother," he said.

Flustered and desperately trying not to show how his words had affected her, she laughed. "Irish blarney won't work on me, Patrick Sullivan. I'm immune to it."

It was his turn to laugh. "It was worth a try." His hands tightened on her shoulders, and he slowly drew her closer. "Brie, I need to say something here."

Did he need to draw her closer to say it? she wondered, knowing another bout of nervousness was claiming her. How was she to keep her wits about her when he was standing so close.

"I...I..." Patrick hesitated. "I want to thank you for the way you've handled all of this." He wasn't certain he could put into words what he was feeling. The emotions were so powerful and he was still struggling to put them all in their proper place. He'd always been a man of deep emotions, and unending loyalty. Perhaps that was why he rarely spoke of his feelings. In his family, it was common, accepted, but he'd never been certain anyone outside the family would be able to understand. Michael and Danny had been lucky, finding women who understand without question the kind of men they were—how important family, loyalty and love were to the Sullivans.

Somehow, he had a feeling Brie did, too. On one level, it pleased him that she seemed to understand his need for his son; on another more personal level, it frightened him because it gave her such power. He couldn't ever forget that this woman had the means to keep him from his son, to rob him of the one thing he held dear above all others.

Learning of Barbara's deception had been crushing, robbing him of the instinctive trust he'd been raised with, the trust that should exist between a man and a woman. He wasn't naive. He'd had far too much experience with women for that, but he also had never been cynical. Until that letter had arrived. Brie's generosity of spirit, the deep abiding love she had for his child, had softened the pain that he'd carried with him since he'd learned of the bittersweet truth.

Sensing that he was struggling with his emotions, Brie sought to soothe his discomfort. She laid a hand to his chest. "Patrick, I know," she said softly, her gaze meeting his. And he realized at that moment, she *did* know. And understood. It was just another bond that seemed to draw them together.

"You've made an almost impossible situation…"

"Possible?" she finished for him, trying to ignore the fact that his hands were slowly drawing her closer to him still.

He grinned. "Yeah. And I appreciate it. We'll just take it slow. Day by day. There's so much I want to know, to show Tommy. I want you both to meet my family—" The panicked look on her face caused him to pause. "What?"

His gaze searched hers and he drew her close enough to smell her sweet scent again.

"Patrick." Her fingers tightened and she licked her dry lips. "I know how important your family is to you, but for now, could we put this off for a bit?" She tried to smile to hide her panic. "I'm afraid I find the idea of meeting them a bit…intimidating, especially because of the circumstances." She couldn't admit that she feared losing even more of her son to Patrick's large family. Nor did she want to think of how they'd feel about her.

"You don't have to worry about my family, Brie. They'll love you and Tommy." Pride came, strong and heartfelt. His family had been the backbone of his life. It was only natural to want to share with them his greatest joy: his son.

But he sensed that his words didn't seem to calm her fears. "But for now, perhaps you're right. We don't want to overwhelm Tommy with too many new people."

"Aye." She nodded in relief.

"Brie." He waited until she tilted her head to look at him. "I want you to know, in spite of the…circumstances that have brought us together, I couldn't want or wish for a more wonderful mother for my child."

"Oh, Patrick." His words surprised her and brought tears to her eyes. She'd not expected them, nor had anyone ever told her she was a wonderful mother. It was a simple comment that had come from the heart, and she found it meant a great deal to her. "Thank you for the sentiment."

"It's true," he said softly, meaning it. "It's not easy raising a child alone. I know. My mother did it, but at least she had my grandfather to help."

"I've h-had Fiona," she stammered, unwilling to admit, perhaps not even to herself, how difficult the road had been. To think of it was far too overwhelming. She'd simply...done what single mothers all over the world had done—let her heart guide her.

"Yes, Brie, you've had Fiona, but there have been a lot of things you haven't had." His meaning was clear. He was speaking of her late husband, but she wouldn't indulge in self-pity. She couldn't. "A lot of things you've had to give up because of Tommy." His gratitude seemed to come in waves.

"Aye," she admitted softly, suddenly feeling weary over the entire day's events.

"I'd...I'd like to help fill in the gaps, if you'll let me."

She knew what he was offering, and for a moment her heart leapt at the thought, but her practical mind halted her wayward emotions.

"Patrick." She had to choose her words very carefully. She didn't want him to know how much his offer tempted or frightened her. "I appreciate your offer. Sincerely. And I'm sure Tommy will be pleased to have his father around." She'd keep things on this distant level, relate everything to Tommy and keep Patrick in his proper place. "It's your relationship with *him* that's important," she reminded him. "He needs you." She wanted the situation very clear. "I've no need for anything." She'd been telling herself the same thing for so long, she could almost believe it.

Feeling rebuffed on some basic masculine level, Patrick's eyes narrowed and the urge to prove her words wrong was immediate.

"I can think of a great many things you need," he returned quietly, drawing her suddenly stiff body closer. "A helping hand now and again," he whispered, lifting his thumb to stroke her cheek, and watching her eyes widen in absolute alarm. "Someone to share the day's troubles and triumphs with." His thumb drifted to her mouth, dragging slowly over her succulent lower lip, wondering what she'd taste like. "A shoulder to cry on." His voice had dropped to a husky whisper. "A hand to hold in the dark of night."

Mesmerized by his soft, hypnotic words, and his gentle, sensuous touch, she merely stared at him, unable to protest, to move.

"No. No." She shook her head, averting her gaze, unable to keep looking into those startlingly blue eyes, eyes that seemed to see through her, to the secrets she held safely in her heart. "I've no need for—"

"A helping hand when two aren't enough." He tilted her chin up, so she had no choice but to look at him. He saw the panic and sought to soothe her.

The need to taste her, to touch his lips to hers, to ease the ache of curiosity, of desire that had started the moment he'd walked into her shop and laid eyes on her, grew overpowering. A warning echoed in his mind, loud and ominous, but he chose to ignore it as the need clanged louder.

With his eyes still on hers, he slowly leaned down toward her, watching her eyes go wide, her fingers tangling tighter in his sweater.

"Patrick." His name withered out a moment before his lips covered hers.

She'd known it was coming; she'd watched his mouth move toward hers as if in slow motion, and yet she couldn't move. It was as if someone had nailed her shoes to the floor.

She should have been prepared, she realized dully, lifting her hands higher on his broad chest to push him away. Instead, she clung, sliding her hands to his shoulders to steady herself, to draw him closer. But how could she be prepared for a feeling she'd never expected and never experienced?

Shock jolted through her, spiraling into a quick hot ball

of need and desire. It clawed at her, warming her blood, scattering her senses. She moaned softly as Patrick's mouth softly seduced hers, gently leading her deeper and deeper into a dark abyss of emotions she'd never felt before.

How could she not have known that a man's mere…kiss could cause this reaction? How could she not have known what it was like to feel as if you were free-falling off the earth, and didn't care, merely wanting…more, more of this heady, glorious feeling?

Sliding his arms tighter around her, Patrick drew Brie closer. He knew she'd pack a punch; he just hadn't been prepared for the kick that had seemed to rock his world off center the moment his lips had touched hers. The moment the connection had been made, he felt something deep inside of him finally click into place. As if a lock had finally slid home. There was this…connection between them, much more than Tommy, much more than just a physical attraction. It was something even far more primitive and basic.

Something he knew he'd been searching for his whole life.

Ignoring the warning that clanged even louder in his ears, he deepened the kiss, pulling her even closer until he could hear his blood roaring, rushing loudly, drowning out his growing fears. Her body was sweetly curved; her softness meeting his hardness. He heard a soft moan escape her, and knew that he'd dragged them into dangerous waters.

And if he wasn't careful, they'd both drown.

He couldn't risk it. To do so was to risk far more than he could lose. For a fleeting instant, in the recesses of his mind, Patrick wondered if it was already too late.

Reluctantly he drew back from Brie, smiling when she blinked up at him as if coming out of a fog. Her hands had slid down to his chest again, gripping him as if fearing she might fall. He covered them with his own, knowing the moment she fully realized what had happened, she'd probably bolt like a startled deer.

"Patrick." Her breath was still coming far too fast and she had to pause to take a deep breath before continuing. "Patrick," she began again, not certain she liked the gleam of male satisfaction glinting in his eyes. "We can't...we mustn't..."

"We did."

"But we can't," she insisted, lifting a hand to push her hair off her face. She felt flustered and foolish. She was a grown woman with a child. She shouldn't feel like a young, giddy schoolgirl in the throes of her first adolescent crush.

"Never again," she said firmly, sliding her hands free of his and slipping them in her pockets, fearing if she didn't, she'd reach for him again. The need to touch had never seemed so urgent. "We can't let it happen again."

She wanted nothing more than for it to happen again. And again. And then some more. But sanity and reality reared their ugly head. She had to think of Tommy, of the danger this man represented. She couldn't trust a man blindly. She couldn't be a fool or let her heart rule. She had far too much at stake. Her eyes pleaded with him. "Promise me, Patrick." He started to say something, but she didn't let him. "You must promise me, Patrick."

"But, Brie—"

"No." She shook her head, as if she could shake away what had just happened between them. "This is not a good idea and it mustn't ever happen again."

Actually, he thought it was a wonderful idea, but thought it best not to say so. To appease and calm her, he nodded. "All right. I promise, Brie." It was the first lie he could ever remember telling. At least since he was ten and had lied to his mother about who broke her prized lamp.

He went to touch her shoulder, and she shrank back from him. He tried not to let it hurt. "I'm sorry." He wasn't sorry in the least.

She let out a relieved breath, too wrapped up in her own intense feelings to realize his voice lacked conviction. "No need to apologize, Patrick." She shrugged, trying to make light of it. "I'm sure it's nothing more than the emotions of the day." She had to find some reason for this... madness, some excuse for her to forget, even for a moment, her obligations and responsibilities.

"Of course," he agreed, not believing it for a moment. But he saw no need to point that out to her, not now when she was so rattled. He'd have to give her time, he realized. Time to get used to him, time to accept this incredible...connection between them. But now was not the time. He glanced over her head at the mantel clock. "I'd best be going." Distance would do them both some good, he decided. He needed some time to think, to sort out all the events of the day, to put things in perspective.

She let out a relieved sigh. "Fine, then. I'll see you tomorrow, around five?" She had no idea how she was going to handle him being part of her everyday life. It frightened her more than anything in a good, long while.

He nodded. "Good night, Brie."

She refused to look into those blue eyes. She was far too unsettled from his kiss. "Good night."

Quietly she shut the door after him, then leaned against it and closed her eyes. Her lips were still warm from his. If she concentrated, she could remember every feeling, every sensation that had battered her senses the moment his lips—those soft, wonderful, magical lips—had touched hers.

She lifted a hand to her mouth. It couldn't happen again.

Not now. Not ever. The decision made sense, and yet for some reason made her heart ache.

She'd agreed to let Patrick into Tommy's life. But if she let him kiss her again, she'd be letting him into her heart, as well.

Brie shivered, knowing it was something she could never, ever allow to happen.

If it did, it could cost her her son.

Chapter Six

Patrick Sullivan was born to be a father, Brie thought with a smile as she washed the last of the dinner dishes. Patrick was busy giving Tommy his bath, and she could hear her son's high-pitched giggles all the way in the kitchen. It tickled her heart.

By the end of the first week, Patrick had become a firm presence in their lives. Now, after three weeks, he was firmly entrenched in their daily routines, so much so that at times, it was hard to remember what life had been like before Patrick Sullivan had arrived on their doorstep.

True to his word, Patrick had spent as much time as possible with Tommy, relieving her of a great many duties and responsibilities.

Dipping a pot into the soapy water, Brie glanced out the window. She hated to admit it, but free time was a luxury she'd come to look forward to. Having time to herself was something she'd not had in a long, long time.

Still working midnights, Patrick would arrive at the shop right about lunchtime with either some delicious carryout, or a care package of wonderful home-cooked food from his mother. He'd have lunch with Tommy, then drive him to his play group, returning afterward to pick the child up. While Brie worked in the store in the afternoons, Patrick tended to Tommy, taking him to the park, the zoo or merely playing with him upstairs.

After she closed the shop, they'd have dinner together, all of them, and then Patrick would play with Tommy, bathe him, and then stay until he was asleep for the night, before heading off to work.

Brie's smile widened when she thought of how quickly and firmly attached Tommy had become to his father. It warmed her heart and made her gratitude for Patrick seem boundless. Tommy seemed to be blossoming under Patrick's loving care and attention, and to her surprise, she found very little resentment at sharing her boy. Perhaps because Patrick had made the child so happy. She'd made the right decision, she realized, in spite of all her fears— fears that had seemed magnified when Patrick had first come into her life. Now, they seemed almost...foolish.

"So the boys are having their bath," Fiona said, coming into the kitchen with a wide grin. She'd taken to calling Patrick and Tommy "the boys." If Brie worried about how Fiona would accept Patrick into their lives, she had no fear. Fiona, like Tommy, was totally besotted with him.

"And enjoying it from the sounds of it," Brie said, shutting off the faucet and setting the pan in the drain. She turned to Fiona, and then frowned. "And where are you off to now?" Every evening, Fiona had been stepping out. At first, Brie was certain she was merely doing it to give them all time to adjust to the situation, now she wasn't so sure. "And is that another new dress you're wearing?" One brow rose and Brie tried not to smile.

"Not so new," Fiona protested, running a hand down

the skirt she hoped was flattering. "I bought it a few weeks ago."

"Aye, I see." Brie bit back a smile. "And where is it you're off to on a night like this?" Brie glanced out the window. The end of October was drawing near. The weather had deteriorated to bitter winds and bone-chilling temperatures. The promise of snow hung heavy in the air.

"I've...a date," Fiona said, cursing the faint blush that heated her cheeks.

Brie's head whipped around and her eyes widened. "A...date?" She wasn't certain if this news pleased or frightened her. "With a man?"

Fiona bristled, smoothing back her hair with a gnarled hand. "And that surprises you, does it?" Indignation sounded in her voice. "I'm old, lass, not dead."

Immediately contrite, Brie laid a hand on Fiona's arm. "I'm sorry. I didn't mean—"

Fiona laughed. "Yes, you did, but that's all right. I'm going to an Irish pub in Logan Square to listen to some music." She shrugged, trying to make light of it. "I've met some new friends, and they've invited me to join them."

Pleased, Brie smiled. "That's lovely, Fiona. Really." She gave the woman's arm an affectionate squeeze, grateful that she'd found something to give her pleasure in life. Now that Patrick was around to help, it seemed as if they both had plenty of extra time. Something else she felt indebted to Patrick for. She'd always felt guilty that Fiona had spent all of her time with her, working in the shop or with Tommy. Now the woman was finally beginning to step out and enjoy herself once in a while, and nothing could have pleased Brie more. "But please do be careful," she cautioned, glancing out the window again in worry. "It's a wicked night out."

"Aye, girl, careful I always am."

"Brie! Brie! I need some reinforcements." Patrick's deep voice rang through the house. "And a few more towels wouldn't be bad, either."

Laughing, Brie shook her head. "I can't imagine what the two of them have gotten into now."

"You'd best go see, then." Fiona bent and kissed her cheek. "And I'd best be off before I'm late." She smoothed her hair down one more time.

"Brie!" Patrick's voice sounded panicked. "Help!"

Brie hurried out of the kitchen, stopping at the linen closet to grab a stack of towels, wondering what on earth Patrick had done with the ones she'd already left for him.

She knocked on the bathroom door. "Patrick, I've got your towels."

"Come in," he called, then cautioned, "But you'd better duck. And step high," he added with a laugh as the door slowly creaked open.

Curious and amused, Brie's eyes widened in shock as the breath roared out of her in a whoosh. She froze just inside the doorway.

The room was hot and steamy. The tub was full almost to the brim with water which was sloshing over the edge, bubbling over to spill on the floor. Small, colorful plastic boats, planes and cars bobbed about. She ignored all of it as her gaze fastened on Patrick. The towels in her arms slipped unheeded to the floor.

The man was naked!

Stark raving, Mother of Mercy naked!

She thought her heart was going to jump out of her chest.

Except for a small, damp towel he had wrapped around his waist, the man didn't have a stitch on. She swallowed hard. The towel he wore dipped dangerously low on his narrow hips, barely skimming the top of his muscled thighs.

Her throat was suddenly incredibly dry, making speech impossible.

Dressed, Patrick Sullivan was a sight to behold. Naked, he was...breathtaking. It would be a miracle if she didn't faint.

She couldn't seem to prevent her gaze from slowly skimming the length of him. His black hair was drenched and plastered tight against his head, only emphasizing his beautiful eyes and incredible face. His shoulders were broad, his chest dusted with a patch of thick, dark hair that glistened with beads of water and narrowed to an enticing vee just where the towel started and her imagination began.

She blinked, once, twice, trying to clear the vision of what was hidden under that towel as her gaze traveled the rest of the length of him. His legs were long, muscled and well shaped. Water lapped around his calves.

"Ma-ma!" Giggling and naked as a jaybird, Tommy squirmed in Patrick's loving arms, dragging her out of her reverie. "Wet!" He giggled again, squirming to break free of Patrick's arms, extending one chubby arm toward her. "Bath, Ma-ma?" He waved his arms and kicked his feet as if inviting her to join them.

She just kept staring at Patrick.

He shifted his weight, totally unfazed by the blush that touched her cheeks. He shrugged, tightening his grip on the squirming bundle in his arms.

"I figured it would be easier, and a lot more fun to give him his bath if I just got in the tub with him."

"I...I...see," she stuttered, realizing that was the problem. She *was* seeing. Far too much of this man for her own comfort.

Patrick laughed, shrugging again. "I was going to get wet anyway, so I figured, why not?"

"Why not, indeed." Totally rattled, she dragged a hand

through her hair, trying to look at anything, everything, but him. She couldn't remember the last time she'd seen a near-naked man. If she couldn't remember, she thought in disgust, it had obviously been too long.

"Uh, Brie?" Totally charmed by her embarrassment, Patrick tried not to grin, while keeping a firm grip on his squirming son.

"What?"

"You...uh...dropped the towels."

"Oh?" Embarrassed, she bent and scooped the now-damp towels from the floor. "I'll...I'll...I'll...get some more." She made the mistake of looking at him, and saw the glint of mischief, and amusement, in his eyes. "You did that on purpose, didn't you?" she accused, realizing he'd deliberately flustered her, and not quite certain why.

"Me?" He tried to look innocent and failed miserably. "Now, would I do something like that?" He shifted his body, and the towel seemed to slip a bit, as did her pulse. She was deathly afraid his towel was going to fall.

And deathly afraid it wasn't.

As if he'd read her thoughts, Patrick grinned. It matched his son's. "I do believe you're the one who told me you didn't need...anything." His implication was clear, and she wanted to smack him. On more than one occasion in the past three weeks he'd made a point of reminding her of her ill-chosen words about not needing anything.

"I...I...don't," she stammered, knowing it was a lie. Looking at him in all his naked glory reminded her that perhaps there were a few things in life a woman needed. But she'd die before she ever admitted such a thing to him. Especially now, when he'd made such a point of...proving his point.

She turned and fled from the bathroom, pausing in the hallway to lean against the wall to give her heart and her pulse a chance to calm. Her eyes slid closed. She could still see him, though.

Naked.

Glorious.

Mother of Mercy.

She took another deep breath, pressing her hand to her thrumming heart. She was only human. She might be a mother, but she was also a woman. A woman who had gone far too long without the gentle, much needed touch of a male. It had never bothered her before. In fact, she'd never thought of it, or thought herself the kind of woman who needed a man's touch, until one giant, grinning blackhaired Irishman had roared into her life, turning it upside down, making her wish for things, want things she knew better than to want.

"Brie!" Patrick's voice had her scrambling toward the linen closet, cursing herself for being so foolish. "I'm starting to wrinkle," he complained with a laugh.

She gave her head a shake, trying to dispel her traitorous thoughts. She couldn't think of things other women took for granted. She wasn't any other woman; she didn't have the luxury of indulging herself in fantasies, of wishing for what might be.

She was far too practical and had to deal with the realities of here and now. It was the only way she could hang on to her sanity.

And her battered, war-weary heart.

She had to put Patrick in his proper place. He was Tommy's father. Nothing more. Nothing less.

She couldn't allow him to mean anything to her. She couldn't be touched by the generous love he showered on her boy. She couldn't be swayed by the incredible patience, kindness and caring he displayed toward her. She couldn't let his nearness, his maleness affect her.

And she couldn't forget, not for a moment, that Patrick had the power to take away the most important thing in her life.

Gathering her scattered wits, and strengthening her inner resolve, Brie yanked open the linen closet door and grabbed some fresh towels, then marched back into the bathroom, determined to ignore the man's...body.

He still stood there, grinning like a fool. With her gaze glued on her son, she held out an open towel to scoop her dripping baby boy into her arms.

"Wet!' Tommy caroled, planting a wet sloppy kiss on her cheek.

"Yes, love," she murmured, wrapping the towel securely around him, and ignoring Patrick and his near-nakedness. "I can see that."

"Drink?" He pressed his nose close to hers. His eyes filled with a charm all his own.

She laughed. "I think you've had enough water for one night, son." Deliberately ignoring Patrick, she marched back out of the bathroom. She heard his soft laughter follow her, and began muttering a string of muted curses under her breath.

"More candy? Pease?" Tommy begged a week later. Snuggled between Patrick and Brie watching a Disney movie, with only a roaring fire lighting the room, Tommy rose to his knees, then lifted a hand to Patrick's face. "Pease?"

Patrick was slouched comfortably on the couch, legs atop the coffee table, one arm protectively around Tommy, the other draped along the top of the couch. Next to him, but with Tommy a careful barrier between them, Brie sat in the corner, her legs curled under her in comfort. She'd felt more relaxed these past few weeks than she could ever remember.

At her son's question, she turned toward him. "You've had more than enough candy for one night, love," Brie scolded, glancing at Patrick over Tommy's head, a look of warning in her eyes. Since Halloween, when Patrick had taken Tommy trick-or-treating, dressed like Oscar the Grouch, with Tommy in a matching Grouch outfit, making them look like mismatched twins, the little imp had been begging for candy like a piker nearly every hour on the hour.

Sensing he wasn't getting anywhere with her, Tommy flashed Brie a quick, charming smile, which he then turned on his unsuspecting father.

"Pease, Da?" he begged pitifully. "Da, pease candy?" Pressing his nose to Patrick's, Tommy patted his father's face with candy-sticky hands, his eyes pleading as only a two-year-old can do.

Da.

The word hung in the air for a long, silent moment. Then Patrick's stunned gaze met Brie's.

"He...he called me...Da." Patrick's voice, his eyes, were filled with pure emotion that brought an unexpected warmth to Brie's heart. Patrick took such joy, such unabashed pleasure in everything their son did. It was a pleasure for her to watch, reminding her of how right her decision had been to allow him into his son's life.

Tommy was better for it, she knew.

"I know." She beamed at her son, pleased beyond measure, even if he was a sneaky little scoundrel who was merely trying to charm more candy out of his poor father.

"Da," Patrick repeated in awe, grabbing Tommy around the waist and hauling him into his lap. "You finally know who I am." He laughed, thrilled, cradling the boy man-style in his lap.

Patrick lifted the top of Tommy's "Sesame Street" pajamas and blew a series of raspberries that made Tommy screech wildly and bellow in laughter. Realizing he'd done something to please, Tommy began repeating the word over and over again, delighting Patrick.

"Yep, I am definitely your da." Patrick hadn't realized how important the word was or how much he needed to hear it. Until this moment. Each and every day, his son did something unexpected, something that caused his already full heart to expand even farther with love.

"Candy?" Still giggling, Tommy reached for Patrick, snuggling closer to his warmth. Patrick cradled his son in his arms, then snuck a glance at Brie, before sliding his hand into the little white bag of black licorice on the couch.

"I saw that," Brie said with a smile.

"No, you didn't." Patrick grinned at her as he slipped the piece of candy into his son's mouth.

"Aye, I did. You're spoiling him, Patrick Sullivan," she accused, but the words held no temper, only affection.

"I am," Patrick agreed amiably, sneaking another piece of candy into his own mouth.

Brie glanced at him, her eyes twinkling in amusement. "And you're both going to rot out your teeth if you don't stop eating that stuff." Both Patrick and Tommy had an affection for the sweet, sticky stuff. Just one of many things they had in common. She reached for the bag, starting a virtual tug of war with Patrick.

"Mine," he declared, mimicking one of Tommy's favorite sayings, and giving the bag a tug.

"Share," she returned with a grin, giving the bag a tug of her own, vividly aware that Tommy was watching the goings-on with interest. The child had never seen the interplay between a man and a woman before Patrick had entered their lives, and from the look on the boy's face, it obviously fascinated and delighted him.

Dennis had kept a careful distance from her and Tommy. He'd never shared anything with them, deliberately leaving the room if they entered.

Over the four weeks, she'd come to enjoy doing even the simplest things with Patrick and her son, things that had given Tommy a brief glimpse of normalcy, of what a mother *and* a father were all about. She'd always feel grateful to Patrick for giving her boy—their boy—that.

Patrick gave the bag another tug. "You don't even like licorice."

"True." She wrestled the bag free from him. "But you two like it far too much."

"Your mother took our candy," Patrick accused, looking at Tommy. The movie flickered on the screen. The credits rolled by, unwatched.

"Tattletale," Brie muttered under her breath, enjoying the family atmosphere Patrick's presence had added to their life. It was the kind of family life she'd always wanted for her son.

"Ma-ma, candy?" Tommy stood up, reaching one arm to loop around Patrick's neck, while the other reached for Brie, drawing them close, making a kid sandwich out of him. "Kiss!" he demanded, bouncing on his bare feet. "Kiss! Kiss!"

Thinking her son wanted a kiss, Brie leaned forward to plant a loud, smacking kiss to the imp's chubby cheek. But he moved back, and she found her mouth hovering millimeters away from Patrick's. She froze.

"Kiss!" Tommy demanded, watching them with a grin.

"You heard the kid," Patrick whispered. "It's too late to back out now." He didn't give her a chance. He closed the distance between them, covering her mouth gently with his.

She had been absolutely certain she'd forgotten what his kisses felt like. She'd tried to banish the memory, even though it had given her more than a few sleepless nights. But the moment his mouth touched hers, the memory, the flavor, the feelings all came rushing back, swamping her.

He tasted of licorice, and something faintly forbidden— what, she couldn't quite remember at the moment since her brain had ceased to function.

When he reached across Tommy, to cradle her face in his hands, she heard a sigh of pleasure and realized it was her own.

She was sitting on a sturdy sofa, so why did the earth feel as if it had dipped under her?

Her thoughts spun until she couldn't think, only feel the wonderful, glorious sensations that overtook her common sense. She couldn't wonder or fear why it felt so right, so perfect, so utterly…natural to have his hand on her cheek, his lips on hers. She couldn't question why she suddenly felt complete, as if she'd finally been given a gift she'd been yearning for, for far too long.

She could do nothing but respond honestly, openly.

"Me kiss!" Tommy was bouncing again, pressing his face against theirs, wanting to be included.

Reluctantly Patrick drew back and smiled, pleased at the soft glow of desire shadowing Brie's eyes.

"Dirty pool," she muttered, making him grin.

"Spoilsport," he countered, pleased as well by the fact that he'd taken her by surprise. Courtesy of his son, he thought with affection. She'd been too stunned to protest, to tell him again what she didn't need.

He stared at her for a moment. She might not think she needed him. But her eyes told a different story.

She wanted him.

He had enough experience with women to recognize the signs, but it wasn't enough, he realized. It wasn't enough for her to just want him. Wanting could be, and usually was, temporary. He was beginning to realize he wanted—needed—something far more permanent from her.

It scared him, but not nearly as much as the thought that some day he could lose her. She could meet someone, remarry, and then what?

He'd been thinking about it a lot. What would that do to his relationship with her? More important, with Tommy. It caused fear, he realized, a fear unlike any he'd known since the day he'd received the letters telling him of Tommy's birth.

It would have been bad enough to never know of his son, worse to know him, love him, and then lose him again. He didn't think he could bear it. Nor did he think he would be able to feel comfortable about their situation or the fact that if Brie chose to remarry, he might lose his son. She still had that power. He had to find a way to neutralize it, without hurting any of them.

Knowing she wanted him was a start. However small, it was something to build on. He didn't want to admit that the thought of Brie marrying, of her being with another man, haunted him, worrying his days.

He was glad she wanted him, not that she'd ever admit it.

And he couldn't tell her he knew. Not yet. She'd be frightened, and he would do nothing to shatter the fragile bond of trust they'd developed during all these weeks.

No, he'd have to be patient and bide his time. And hopefully, he'd have luck—and perhaps a little of his son's help—to smooth the way so they could make things a bit

more permanent, and give him the peace of mind he so
sorely needed.

"Kiss, Da?"

"Any time, kid." Patrick obliged his son, planting loud,
smacking kisses all over his face until the baby was giggling helplessly. Breathless and rubbing his eyes, Tommy
snuggled closer into his father's arms.

"Grouch," Tommy muttered, sticking a thumb in his
mouth as he squirmed for comfort. His lashes slid closed
for a moment.

Patrick glanced at Brie. "I think he's had it for the
night." He brushed the hair off Tommy's face. "Why don't
I go tuck him in and get him the Grouch."

"Fine." Still rattled from his kiss, Brie rose. "I'll rewind
the movie and clean up a bit." She reached for the half-
empty bowl of popcorn they had shared, and the forgotten
bag of candy that now sat forlornly on the end of the couch.

"Let's go, imp." Patrick rose with Tommy in his arms.
It was hard to believe how much he knew of his son's life,
his routine already. There was a time, not so long ago,
when he yearned greedily for this knowledge. Now he
hugged it to him, every precious insight a rare and special
gift. A gift Brie had generously given to him.

"Sing, Da?"

Walking to the kitchen, Brie grinned, knowing Patrick
would sit in the rocker and croon to their boy until he was
fast asleep. Not the same, heart-sad melody her father had
crooned to her, but one from his own family memories, one
just as sad, lonely and heartfelt.

Sometimes she just sat on the couch and watched him,
gently rocking Tommy, holding their son in his arms, his
eyes and heart unguarded as he relished the simple pleasure
of crooning his son to sleep.

He was touching her heart, she realized with a panic, as

she dumped the balance of the popcorn in the trash. Somehow, when she wasn't looking, he'd been touching and healing the parts of her she'd thought shattered forever.

It was a surprise to learn they weren't.

But it didn't change anything, Brie decided with firmer resolve as she placed the empty bowl in the sink and paused to stare out at the dark night.

She would never—could never—allow him into her heart.

Winter arrived with a vengeance near the end of November, dropping the temperatures and dumping a thick blanket of snow all over the Midwest.

With Thanksgiving just days away, Brie was busier than usual at the shop. The Christmas rush seemed to be coming earlier and earlier. If this kept up, she'd have to hire a part-time clerk, because even with Fiona's help, she couldn't handle the volume.

Looking up from the packages she was wrapping for a customer, she glanced out the window. It was almost dark, the day almost done. She hadn't stopped from the moment she'd opened the doors this morning. The weather had turned cold, not bitter yet, but cold enough to warrant dragging out winter clothing. More snow had begun falling almost three hours ago, accumulating on the sidewalk and snarling traffic in front of the shop.

Usually she loved the first days of snow, and would spend hours sitting at one of the windows in the apartment, staring in amazement at God's miracle. With a cup of hot cocoa, a fire roaring at her back, and Tommy safely snuggled asleep in his crib, nothing was more comforting or soothing to her.

Thinking of Tommy, she frowned suddenly, rubbing her

throbbing temples. She was glad she'd bundled him into his new snowsuit and winter boots this morning.

With a sigh, she glanced at her watch, grateful Patrick was picking Tommy up from his play group today. She had no idea how she would have managed the past week without him. Although she was grateful for all the additional business, it severely cut into her time with Tommy, putting more and more of a burden on Patrick, something she felt immensely guilty for.

When she'd tried to apologize this morning, he'd brushed away her concerns, insisting it didn't bother him a bit. She believed him, but still, the guilt came.

"Are you ready for Thanksgiving?" Mrs. Cole, one of her regular customers, asked, interrupting her thoughts just as she put the finishing touches on a bright gold package.

"I'm almost ready," she hedged, rubbing a spot of tension at the base of her neck. She'd nearly winced at the mention of Thanksgiving. It was two days away and she'd yet to shop, plan or prepare anything.

"It's hard when you work and have a family," Mrs. Cole said, examining the gaily wrapped package with a discerning eye.

"At times," Brie admitted, forcing a smile she didn't feel. She was tired and a bit more weary than normal, and her throat felt scratchy for some reason. "Your packages are all finished." Accepting the grateful woman's credit card, Brie quickly finished the transaction and wished the woman a happy holiday.

As soon as the door shut behind Mrs. Cole, Brie went into her office and pulled a bottle of aspirins out of her desk, quickly swallowing them down with her coffee, which was now cold. She'd been so busy she hadn't had time for lunch or to make fresh coffee.

The tinkling of the shop bell sent her hurrying toward the front again with a weary sigh.

She heard Tommy's belt-busting giggle just as she came through the door of the shop.

"We're back," Patrick called, cradling a straining Tommy in his arms. She had to grin at the sight they made. Patrick's dark hair was dotted with fresh snowflakes as was his leather jacket. The cold had put twin flags of color in his cheeks and his ear-to-ear grin matched his son's.

Tommy, bundled up in his new, stiff snowsuit with matching boots, looked like a starched snowman as he leaned out of Patrick's arms, giggling. In his little fist, he had a mangled bunch of drooping daisies.

"Ma-ma," Tommy called, waving the distressed daisies in the air like a flag. "Pe-sent." His tiny fist waved faster in her general direction.

"A present? For me?" Her gaze went to Patrick's. "They're lovely." She rescued the drooping blooms from her son's sticky fist, then inhaled deeply of their sweet scent, wondering where Patrick had found them in the cold of winter.

"He tried to eat them," Patrick said with a laugh, looking at her for a long moment. She looked pale and drawn to him. It instantly concerned him. "So I had to… improvise," he admitted with a wicked grin. That grin made her tender heart tumble over in her chest. The man's smile ought to be outlawed!

"Improvise?" Grinning, Brie moved closer and gave her son's little mouth, which had a sticky, suspicious-looking mustache, a motherly sniff. "Licorice again, love?" she asked with a raised brow.

Tommy grinned, revealing two teeth covered with telltale black stains. " More candy?" Kicking his feet in excitement, Tommy looked at his father hopefully, wrapping one arm tighter around his neck to speak directly against his face. "Candy, pease?"

"He's got your number, Patrick Sullivan," Brie said with a laugh, knowing neither she nor Patrick could resist that irresistible look on her son's face. She began untying Tommy's hood. It was damp with snow. She reached for her tissue from her pocket and wiped his drippy nose. "No more candy for you, love," she said, giving the baby a kiss on his cheek as she pulled off his hood and ruffled his hair. "You'll ruin your dinner."

"Dogs?" he asked hopefully, his eyes shining.

Brie shook her head. "'Fraid not. No hot dogs tonight, sport."

"Damn." Woeful, Tommy hung his head as Brie gaped at his...new vocabulary word.

Her surprised gaze went from Tommy to Patrick, who flushed bright red and started laughing as he clamped a hand over his son's mouth, then bent to whisper in his ear.

"Shh, son, you're going to get us both in trouble. I told you not to say that word."

Obviously delighted with his new vocabulary word, Tommy grinned. "Damn. Damn. Damn." Each word was punctuated with a little pat on his father's cheek, and a kick of his little boot.

Sheepishly, Patrick looked at Brie, deciding he'd better explain. "I...uh...guess...he heard me...say..."

Brie was trying hard not to grin. "I...uh...get the picture, Patrick."

"It was a mere slip of the tongue," he defended, still grinning and ruining the whole effect.

Tommy turned to his father with a pleading expression. "Dogs?"

Brie shook her head. After tucking the bouquet under her arm, she began unzipping Tommy's snowsuit. If she didn't take it off before Patrick set him down, the boy would topple over from the weight.

"No hot dogs for dinner tonight," she repeated, realizing her son still had a one-track mind when it came to food.

"Uh…Brie?"

The tone of Patrick's voice, and his decided fidgeting had her looking up.

"What?" She narrowed her gaze on him, suddenly suspicious. "What!" She sighed, slipping her hands in the pockets of her slacks, something he'd noticed she did every time she got nervous. Or he got too near.

"Uh…I…uh…don't…think Tommy's asking for…hot dogs."

"Well, of course he is," she said, then made the mistake of glancing at Patrick's face. Brie's maternal alarm went off at such a high pitch it was loud enough to go off the scale. "If he's not asking for hot dogs…" Her voice trailed off in horror. "Oh, my word." She pressed a hand to her throbbing temple and prayed for patience. "Patrick, please, *pul-lease,* tell me you didn't buy him a…dog?"

Dogs were Tommy's latest, greatest passion and every time he saw one he fell hopelessly in love. And Patrick was absolutely no help. He was just as besotted.

Trying to look clearly offended, Patrick drew himself upward. "I most certainly did *not* buy him a dog. You told me specifically I couldn't buy him a dog. Remember?"

"Yes, I most certainly remember." Brie's breath came out in a whoosh of relief. She absolutely, positively did not need something else to take care of, especially something that had to be walked or fed during the night.

"Now we wouldn't do anything your mother said we couldn't, would we, son?" Patrick was speaking to Tommy, but the words were intended for her.

Brie's gaze shifted from one guilty face to the other.

They wore matching grins of such mischievousness she immediately knew something was up.

Cradling Tommy closely in his arms, Patrick rocked back on his heels, looking supremely pleased with himself. "I most assuredly did not buy him a dog," he repeated with a grin. "Danny and Katie *gave* him one."

Oh, Mother of Mercy! She had to have misunderstood. She had to have heard wrong. She stared at Patrick blankly for a moment, hoping she'd heard wrong.

"Katie and Danny gave Tommy one…what?" She blinked up at him. Her head was pounding louder now, and it felt as if someone was scratching a rusty blade up and down her throat.

"Oh, my word." She shook her head. "Patrick Sullivan, did you or did you not get this child a dog?" She shook her finger at him, much the same way she would have Tommy. "And don't confuse the issue with whether you exchanged money for it or not."

Looking crestfallen, Patrick tried to explain. "I did, but I couldn't help it, Brie," he rushed on, clearly realizing he might have made a tad error in judgment. "You should have seen Tommy's face. I took him over to the day-care center and little Molly's dog just had brand-new puppies and…"

She sighed, trying not to roll her eyes. "Molly?"

"Katie and Danny's little girl."

"Danny being one of your…older brothers, the one who's married to your sort-of-adopted, but not really your sister, Katie?" she asked, trying to keep the family relationships clear.

Still grinning, he nodded. "Not to be confused with Michael, my oldest brother, who's married to Joanna, and has a daughter Emily, as well as triplet boys."

She whacked him on the arm. "Don't confuse the issue,

and don't confuse me." She was going to have a hard time keeping track of all the Sullivans without a regulation scorecard.

Amused, Patrick rubbed his arm. "I was just trying to be helpful," he defended with a smile.

"Just help me a little less, here."

Brie rubbed her throbbing temples. Her headache was getting worse, and she also felt slightly nauseated. Maybe it was just from lack of food, she reasoned, since she had missed lunch. And breakfast. She longed for a hot meal and a long, blissful night of sleep.

She sighed heavily. "All right, finish this story, Patrick. Explain to me, please, exactly why we now have a…dog." She could barely get the word out. Instinct had her glancing behind him, looking for the offending creature. "And where is he?"

"She," Patrick corrected, making her groan again. "It's a girl." He wondered if Brie realized she'd used the term *we*. For some reason it pleased him immensely to know she was thinking of them as a unit.

"Wonderful," she said glumly. "It gives me something to look forward to, since female puppies have a tendency to want to produce offspring." Just the thought made her want to cry. She did not need this. She definitely did not need this. Especially today when she felt so…tired, cranky and just so overwhelmed. "So where is this…puppy?"

"Still at Katie's." He grabbed her arm to prevent her from fleeing back into her office. "Here's what I figure. The puppy's too young to be taken from her mother yet, but when she's ready, I'll just bring her to my house. You won't have to worry about taking care of it or anything."

She narrowed her gaze to look at him suspiciously. "Now why does that sound wonderful in theory, but putting it into practice might take some…effort."

She didn't want to think about all the implications of having Tommy's puppy at Patrick's. She'd deliberately avoided meeting Patrick's family yet, simply because it was…intimidating. Not just because of the circumstances that had brought she and Patrick together, but simply because of the size of the Sullivans. There were just so many of them, and she secretly feared losing her son to Patrick's enormous—and a bit overwhelming—family.

"Brie?" Patrick lifted a hand and cupped her cheek, caressing her in a soothing gesture that instantly made her regret her sharp words. In spite of the coldness of the day, his hand was still warm and she felt her skin tingle from the contact. "Rough day?" he asked.

She had no idea where the tears came from, or why, but they instantly filled her eyes and she felt her shoulders slump.

"I'm…just tired I guess." The gentleness of his touch, the concern in his voice had brought all of her feelings flooding to the surface. Having a headache and sore throat didn't help, either.

"Brie…" Patrick let the word trail off as his finger continued to gently stroke her tender skin.

After all this time, he'd gotten to know Brie and her habits and schedule very well. He knew how hard she worked at managing all the different aspects of her life in order to keep things running smoothly. Yet, she still gave Tommy one hundred percent of herself and her attention, no matter how busy or tired she was. He had no idea how she handled everything as well as she did.

He'd found his initial admiration growing for her, as well as the inexplicable feelings that had surfaced the moment he'd laid eyes on her. He'd tried to contain them, but couldn't. He was beginning to worry about the way he was feeling about Brie. It scared the hell out of him.

"Did you have lunch?" he finally asked with a frown, noting how pale she looked. He juggled Tommy in his other arm to keep him occupied. Instinct had his arms aching to hold Brie, to kiss away the furrowed lines between her brows.

She shook her head and managed a wan smile. "I haven't had breakfast yet," she said, deciding to make a joke of it. She pushed her hair off her face and blew out an exasperated breath. "I've been so busy, I just haven't had time."

The bell tinkled behind Patrick and Tommy, and Brie groaned.

"Oh, Brie?" Mrs. Cole called, waving the wrapped packages in the air.

Brie knew the fussy Mrs. Cole probably wanted her packages rewrapped for some unknown reason. She wanted to cry again.

"Brie, look. You take care of your customer. I'll take care of Tommy and dinner. At five, when you close the shop, just come upstairs." Patrick trailed a finger down her nose in an affectionate gesture, wanting only to soothe the worry from her face. "Tommy and I will handle everything from here on out."

"But—" Her attention divided between Mrs. Cole and Patrick, she was stunned when Patrick leaned down and brushed a quick kiss across her lips.

"No arguing. You're tired and it takes too much energy. We'll see you at five." He gave her another kiss, then was out the door with Tommy before she could open her mouth.

For a long moment, she stood there, stunned, staring after him, drooping daisies still in her hands. Lifting her fingers to her mouth, she could still feel the warmth of Patrick's lips, could still taste him. Her heart was just now settling down from the riot his kiss had brought on.

"Brie?" Mrs. Cole was standing in front of her, waving a hand in the air to get her attention. "Are you in there? Brie!"

Startled, Brie jumped. She placed a hand to her still-thrumming heart and blinked up at Mrs. Cole.

Lord, the man was scrambling what was left of her senses.

Chapter Seven

At exactly one minute to five, Brie locked the shop and dragged herself upstairs. Not certain she could deal with another one of Patrick's surprises—if the new dog was any indication—she hesitantly unlocked the front door to the apartment, expecting to find Tommy and Patrick rolling around the floor, playing.

The house was quiet. With some concern, she went from room to room, wondering what was going on. There was no one home. She had just come out of her bedroom where she'd eyed the bed lovingly, wishing she was in it, when someone knocked on the door.

Rubbing her forehead, she slipped off her shoes and went to answer the door. A grinning Patrick stood there.

"You look beat," he said by way of invitation, brushing past her to come into the apartment, bringing with him his own special masculine scent. It always lingered in the air, long after he'd gone home, reminding her of him and his presence in her life. She wondered just when she'd stopped resenting it.

Apparently he'd been home. He'd showered and changed, and now wore a crisp pair of jeans, another white pullover sweater and a different leather coat. This one was full-length, and made him look like one of the strong, swaggering heroes from an Old West movie. "Where's Tommy?" she asked in alarm, noting his arms were empty.

"My mother, Katie and Joanna have kidnapped him for the night."

"I see," she said stiffly, wondering when he'd started making decisions for her, and trying hard not to resent it.

"No, you don't," Patrick said with a smile. "I thought you could do with a night off." He laid a hand on her cheek again, much the same way he'd done this afternoon. She wanted to move away from his touch, but she was too tired. And his touch, so filled with concern, ruffled something deep inside of her. It had been a long time since anyone had touched her. She was trying not to be charmed. Oh, if she wasn't careful, the things this man could do to her heart.

Grateful, she finally managed a smile, pushing back her own thoughts. "Thanks. That was very kind of you." She cocked her head to look at him, her eyes shining. "But I suspect this is more of a peace offering."

"Peace offering?" he said blandly.

"Aye, to get you out of the hot pot about the...dog." She could barely say the word, still unable to believe what he'd done.

"In my business, Brie, I believe it's called a bribe." He grinned, pleased with himself, and wiggled his brows at her. "I'm a cop, remember?"

She let out a long sigh. "Yes, how could I forget, Detective?"

"Are you ready?" he asked, grabbing her coat from its

usual hook and taking her elbow as he pulled her toward the door.

She dug in her heels. "For what?" she cried in alarm.

"Dinner," he said succinctly, turning to her. "Brie, you're exhausted. When I said a night off, I meant it. I thought we'd go to dinner, and maybe take in a flick ourselves. Something to get you to just relax, a night with no worries." He started pulling her along again, to avoid any protests. "Think you can handle a night without anything to do or anything to worry about?"

She grinned, relaxing. "I think I can manage." The idea sounded decadent and totally indulgent, but she loved it. He started nudging her toward the door again.

"Patrick!" She came to a halt. "I can't go to dinner like this!"

He looked at her clothing, then at her. "Like what?" he asked, clearly confused.

She sighed. "I've been working in these clothes all day and I look—"

"Beautiful," he said softly. His gaze caught hers, and she saw the softness in his eyes. It made her knees weak and her heart pound. "You look absolutely beautiful," he whispered. The way his eyes went over her made her suddenly feel...beautiful.

She couldn't remember if a man had ever told her she was beautiful before. Certainly not a charmer like Patrick Sullivan, and it pleased her. Immensely. She couldn't help the grin that slid across her face. So, Patrick Sullivan thought she was beautiful. She hugged the knowledge to her guarded heart like a teddy bear.

"Go change," he ordered, glancing at his watch. "Otherwise you won't be able to relax." He tapped his watch. "You've got exactly five minutes, and then I'm coming in and dragging you out, dressed or not."

Feeling he would no doubt do exactly as he said, she didn't bother to argue. She dashed into her bedroom, trying not to think of the glorious night ahead.

"Patrick, if you pour me another glass of wine, I'm going to fall asleep and then you'll have to pick my head up out of the pizza."

He grinned, helping himself to another piece with one hand, while filling her glass with the other.

"Just don't fall on my side." He smiled across the booth at her. "I'm hungry."

With a relaxed sigh, Brie glanced around. Obviously Patrick was well-known in the pizzeria. When they'd come in, several people waved and called to him, and the waitress gave him a big hug and a kiss, making him blush, and, Brie had to admit, her a bit jealous.

They'd been ushered to a cozy, quiet back booth where Patrick had proceeded to order "the usual," which just so happened to have everything she liked on it, as well as a bottle of red wine. She wondered how he knew her so well. He seemed to know her likes, dislikes and, in most ways, they mirrored his own.

As hungry as she was, she'd only managed to consume three of the huge pieces of pizza and a glass and a half of wine, which was a lot for her. Especially considering how tired she was. She wasn't much of a drinker anyway, but when she was tired it seemed to have a stronger effect on her.

"So what made you decide to give me the night off?" she asked. She'd been wondering about it all the way over in the car.

Wiping his mouth with his napkin, Patrick paused, taking a sip of his wine before answering. "Well, I've seen how hard you work and how much you do. You take care of everyone, Brie, but sometimes you forget to take care of yourself.''

She smiled, toying with her wineglass. "Aye, you're right. Sometimes I do forget.'' She shrugged, feeling a bit defensive. "There always seems to be something more important to do.'' She glanced down at the pizza. Staring into those deep blue eyes of his made her knees weak and her head buzz. Patrick Sullivan was a potent masculine specimen, and she might have her defenses up, but she wasn't totally immune to his charm.

She smiled, wanting to broach something she felt guilty about. "You've been a big help to me the past month. Taking Tommy to his play group. Picking him up. Giving him his bath each night. It's been wonderful. For both of us,'' she added softly, startled that she could admit such a thing to him.

She never thought she'd welcome so completely the idea of sharing her son with anyone, but she found not resentment, only simple gratitude.

"I've loved every minute of it,'' Patrick said, putting his napkin down. "I just wish I could spend every minute with him.'' It was a subject he'd been waiting to discuss with her, but he knew how delicate it was and how careful he'd have to be. He had a feeling this wasn't the right time.

She laughed. "And spoil him more than you already do?'' She shook her head. "I don't think that's a good idea. He already has you wrapped around his little finger. All he has to do is bat those big blue eyes and you go all soft on me.'' She grinned. "And don't deny it.''

Patrick laughed. "Guilty as charged. But if you think I'm bad, you have no idea how Da is with him.'' Patrick grew silent for a moment. There was something else he'd been meaning to talk to her about, but had feared bringing up. "Brie, could we talk about…Thanksgiving?''

The mere mention of the holiday had her stiffening in her seat. "Of course, Patrick."

"I know you said you wanted to wait to be introduced to my family and I understand how the situation can be a little awkward for you. But Patrick is my son," he reminded her gently. "And I'd like to spend the holiday with him. And you." His eyes searched hers, and he could see the fear and confusion in them. "I'd like to invite both of you to have dinner at my mother's, with the entire family."

"Thank you, Patrick, for the kind and generous offer." She glanced away for a moment, gathering her thoughts. She wouldn't allow this to threaten her. She couldn't. The decision was hers; he'd given her that. "I appreciate it, I really do. But I don't know if I feel comfortable being introduced to your whole family yet. It's...it's...just so...overwhelming right now, and with the circumstances between us..." She couldn't put into words how she felt about being caught up in Patrick's large, loving family. She'd not met any of the Sullivans simply because she secretly feared their reaction to her, knowing the circumstances of Tommy's birth. It was her own fears and insecurities, and nothing more.

There was another fear, one she didn't want to acknowledge. The fear of losing Tommy, of him getting caught up in a large, loving family, when all she had to offer him was herself. It was childish and she knew it, but still she couldn't ignore the feelings.

"I understand," Patrick said, crestfallen. Brie knew how important his family was to him, but he also understood how important *her* feelings were. He didn't want to do anything to make her uncomfortable, or to disturb the fragile bond of trust they'd built over the past two months. "I just thought it might be nice to spend the holiday with my son."

She couldn't bear to see the disappointment on his face, or hear it in his voice. She smiled, reaching across the table to cover his hand. "And so you should. We'd like very much to invite you to have dinner with us. One Sullivan at a time is all I can handle right now, Patrick."

"I understand." And he did. He knew how intimidating his family could be, and the idea of having Brie and Tommy all to himself was too much of a temptation to pass up.

Thrilled, he squeezed her hand, trying not to notice how beautiful she looked. Or how tired. "I'd love to." He shook his head. "My first real holiday with my son." He held up his finger. "Halloween doesn't count."

Brie laughed suddenly. "Tommy will be overjoyed." She sipped her wine, then yawned. "I'll make a traditional turkey dinner with all the trimmings. As well as homemade pumpkin pie." Immediately she began making a mental grocery list. She hadn't even had time to shop yet. That would take up tomorrow. She tried not to feel overwhelmed by what the next day would bring.

"Are you sure it won't be too much trouble?" he asked. Brie was tired already. And he didn't like the shadows under her eyes. She'd already confessed to having a bit of a sore throat and a headache; he wasn't certain a big holiday dinner was what the doctor ordered.

She laughed. "Holidays are a joyous occasion in our house, Patrick, not work. Please say you'll come?"

"Oh, definitely." He grinned. "I never pass up a free meal." Delighted at the prospect of spending the whole day with Tommy—and Brie—he finished his wine, then looked up at her just as she yawned again. He frowned in concern. "Brie, would you rather skip the movie? I can stop by the video store. We can go home, light a fire, I'll make some popcorn, and you can just curl up on the couch, kick your shoes off and relax.''

''Do I get butter on my popcorn?'' she asked, feeling more relaxed and lighthearted than she had in years and more than grateful for his generous offer.

''As much as you want. I'll even spring for the movie.'' The delight in her eyes and her short little sigh of pleasure at his words was all the answer he needed. He signaled for their bill, paid the waitress, then hustled her out to the car, where she promptly fell sound asleep.

Chapter Eight

A light snow had been falling all night, accumulating on the streets, stalling traffic. The weatherman had predicted nine or more inches before Thanksgiving was over. As Patrick pulled his car to an empty spot in front of Wishes and Whims, he realized he might have to shovel himself out.

Turning up the collar of his coat, he grabbed the flowers he'd brought for Brie, the brightly colored green Nerf ball he'd bought for Tommy, as well as the apple-and-cinnamon pie that Joanna had baked for all of them.

He took the stairs two at a time, anxious to get out of the cold, and inside with Brie and Tommy. With Fiona gone to Michigan with Da, it would just be the three of them. He was looking forward to it. He knocked gently on the door, stamping his feet free of snow, wishing he'd remembered his gloves.

Frowning, he knocked again, wondering why Brie didn't answer. By the third knock, his heart was fluttering with fear.

He'd just lifted his hand to knock again, when the door was slowly pulled open. His mouth fell open in shock.

"Brie!" He pushed through the door, dropping the flowers and the Nerf ball to grab her. "My God, what's wrong?"

She looked...awful. Her hair was a disheveled mess; her eyes were red and bleary. She was dressed in an oversize flannel robe and shivering almost uncontrollably.

"Strep," she managed to get out, placing a hand to her chest as she began to cough. "Tommy got sick late last night. I've been up all night with him." It took a great deal of effort to speak, to breathe. Her throat was on fire, and she felt as if an elephant was sitting on her chest.

Still holding on to her, Patrick kicked the door shut behind him and set the pie down on the floor. He touched her forehead. "You're burning up," he said with a frown, realizing she was just as sick as their son.

She shook her head. "Patrick, please." She had to swallow before she continued, "See to Tommy. I'm fine."

He caught her just as she began to sway, swinging her up in his arms and cradling her close. She was so slight, he could have lifted her with one arm.

"I can see that," he said mildly, trying to disguise his worry as he carried her into her room and laid her gently on the bed. "Where are your blankets?" he asked, looking around the room.

"Tommy's room," she mumbled as she curled into a ball. "I slept on the floor so I could be near him."

He wanted to throttle her. Sleeping on a cold hard wood floor when she was sick? It was a wonder she didn't have pneumonia. He watched as she instinctively snuggled deeper into the bed, and felt an overwhelming wave of helplessness.

Brie wanted to say something to him, then thought better

of it. It was too much of an effort to speak. She wished the pounding in her head would ease. Her entire body ached— every limb, every muscle, every bone. She couldn't remember ever being this tired before.

But Patrick was here now, she thought drowsily. He'd take care of Tommy. She could allow herself to…sleep. Her eyes slid closed and she huddled deeper into the bed, letting relief relax her for the first time in hours.

Satisfied she'd be all right for a minute, Patrick dashed into the baby's room to check on him. Tommy was sleeping peacefully. He dashed back to Brie and tucked a pillow under her head, covering her with a comforter.

"Brie?" He touched her forehead. It was hot, and her cheeks were flushed. She murmured something unintelligible, and curled deeper into the blankets.

Worried, he brushed the hair from her face, and gazed at her. He realized standing here staring at her in a stupor wasn't going to help. What he needed was reinforcements.

Brie woke up groggy, disoriented and cold. She thought of trying to sit up, then thought better of it. Everything hurt. Except her eyes. Without moving her head, she glanced out the window and saw that it was dark. Night. What had happened to the day? she wondered.

Another thought followed, causing fear to shiver over her.

Tommy.

My God, the baby.

Pushing her damp, tangled hair off her face, she took a deep breath, tried to push the covers off so she could climb out of bed. Her legs didn't seem to want to work. She sat up and the room tilted, spun, making her feel as if her stomach was about to empty itself. Her hand went to her head where the throbbing was making her squint. She moaned softly, bringing Patrick into the room on a run.

"So, you're awake." His face creased with worry, Patrick stood over her. From the way he looked, she wondered if the wrong patient was in bed.

"Aye," she managed to get out. "Tommy?"

Patrick smiled. "He's fine and sound asleep. The doctor gave him a shot, and since then he's been doing better. His fever is way down, and he even managed to drink a little soup."

"Doctor?" She blinked. "What doctor?"

"Dr. Summers. The Sullivan family doctor. I called him as soon as I saw how sick you two were." He grinned, tucking the covers under her chin. "He gave you both a shot of antibiotics."

Her eyes flew open. "Some strange…man was poking needles in my bare backside?" Now she understood why her backside ached. Mortified, she closed her eyes again and groaned.

Patrick laughed. "Trust me, Dr. Summers is not strange." He glanced out the window. "I was lucky he came, considering the weather and the holiday."

"The holiday?" Panicked, she tried to sit up, only to have him gently push her back down again. "Oh, Patrick, I'm sorry." Tears blurred her eyes. "I ruined your Thanksgiving."

Laughing, he shook his head. "You didn't ruin it, Brie. Let's just say you made it definitely more interesting." He touched her forehead, relieved she wasn't nearly as hot as this morning. "And there'll be other Thanksgivings."

"But what did you eat?"

He grinned. Only Brie could be sick as a dog, and worried about whether he had food in his stomach or not. "My mother brought over some turkey and stuff. There's plenty left if you're hungry.''

She swallowed hard, praying she was so ill with fever she'd heard him wrong. ''Patrick, did you say...your mother?''

He nodded.

''Oh, Patrick, please, *pul-lease,* tell me you didn't let your mother see me like this?'' Horrified, she wanted to pull the covers over her head and hide.

He laughed. ''Relax, Brie. You're sick. My mother's seen sick people before.''

''Oh, Lord.'' This time she did pull the covers over her head so he couldn't see her tears. She was just so tired and the thought that Patrick's mother had seen her in this condition—weak, ill, unable to care for her own—left her feeling weepy.

Grinning, Patrick peeked under the covers. ''My mother thinks you're adorable, by the way.''

She lifted a hand to swat him and missed.

He laughed, grabbing her hand and kissing it. ''Would you like something? Are you hungry? Thirsty?''

She shook her head. The thought of food made her stomach start to roll. ''Nothing.''

Gently, he peeled the covers off of her so he could see her. ''Brie, honey, why didn't you call me?'' He couldn't tell her the panic he'd felt the moment he arrived and realized just how sick she and Tommy were. If he'd been there sooner, he might have been able to help, to call the doctor before it had gotten so bad.

''It was the middle of the night,'' she whispered, letting her eyes slide closed for a moment to let the panic settle. ''And you were on duty. I didn't want to...bother you.'' She'd never had anyone to call before; had never known the luxury of having someone there when she needed him.

"Doesn't matter." He took her hand in his, wanting her to know he was there. For her. For Tommy. "You shouldn't have gone through this by yourself. You're in no condition to be taking care of anyone."

"I know that now," she admitted, realizing she thought she could ignore her own symptoms in order to see to her child. Her eyes drooped closed. They just seemed too heavy to keep open.

"Go back to sleep," he whispered, kissing her forehead.

"Tommy?"

"Relax." He kissed her again. "I'm here. I'll take care of him, and you. Stop worrying. I'm not going anywhere."

His words drifted through her mind, having a calming effect. Sick as she was, it was a comfort to know Patrick was there. For her. And Tommy.

For the first time in a long time, she felt she could relax. At least for tonight, she wasn't alone. Patrick was here, and until this moment, she hadn't realized how much she truly needed him.

Chapter Nine

The light of dawn was streaming in through the windows. Disoriented, Brie opened her eyes and stretched. The headache was gone finally, and her throat felt slightly better. She wasn't nearly as cold as before. Testing her strength, she sat up slowly. She had to get up to attend to more…pressing matters. Pushing her hair back, she saw the tray of uneaten soup and juice on the floor and smiled. Patrick must have tried to feed her. She didn't remember it. Swinging her legs over the side of the bed, she braced herself and slowly stood, taking a moment to get her bearings. A wave of dizziness hit her for a second, but blissfully passed. Slipping her feet into the slippers Patrick had set by her bed, she gingerly walked out of her room.

In the bathroom, she glanced at her image and nearly grimaced. She was as pale as the moon, and her hair looked like a tangled mop. After bathing her face in some cool water, she pulled a brush through her hair to get it off her face, then pulled it into a ponytail.

Still dressed in her robe, she tiptoed into Tommy's room

to check him. His crib was empty. Feeling a bit panicked, she hurried into the living room, then came to a dead stop, her heart tumbling over in her chest.

Patrick and Tommy were sound asleep on the couch. Patrick had both arms wrapped securely around the sleeping boy, and the imp's head pillowed against his broad chest. Tommy had his father's shirt clutched tightly in one little fist, the other was curled around Patrick's collar.

The sight of them cuddled together, sound asleep, made her heart warm to overflowing and brought tears to her eyes.

Her boys.

She had no idea where the thought came from, or when she'd started thinking of Patrick as hers. She didn't know *when* it came, all she knew was that the feeling was there, bright, new and beautiful.

The feeling terrified her.

As did the knowledge that Patrick had meant it when he said he'd take care of her. And Tommy. That he wasn't going anywhere. Judging from the condition of the living room, which looked as though a small tornado had roared through, he'd been taking care of the baby quite well.

Quietly she went to them, touching Tommy's forehead to check for fever. He was cool as a cucumber and didn't even budge. Patrick's long leg was loped over the top of the couch, and one was hanging off the other end. Their blanket had slipped to the floor. She picked it up and gently covered them with it, bending to kiss them on the cheeks, watching them for a moment, certain she'd never seen a more beautiful sight. The memory stayed with her as she returned to bed, and dreamed of her lovely boys.

The smell of food woke her up, and the sound of Tommy's giggling. Opening her eyes, Brie lay still for a moment, letting her body adjust to wakefulness.

She sat up slowly, and glanced out the window. It was daylight. Gingerly getting out of bed, she followed her nose and the noise into the kitchen.

"Ma-ma!" Tommy squealed from his high chair, banging his fists on the top. Obviously delighted to see her, he grinned a toothless grin, then picked up his cup and began to drink. Milk dribbled out the sides and drooled down his chin.

"Good morning," she said, going to her son to brush the top of his head and kiss it. She glanced at Patrick. "You look good wearing scrambled eggs," she said with a smile. Patrick's hair and shirt were dotted with Tommy's breakfast.

"We...uh...were sort of having a—"

"Spit?" Tommy blew out his cheeks and let loose a volley of eggs that flew through the air, landing on the table and Patrick. The baby clapped his hands in glee.

One brow rose as Brie looked at Patrick, trying not to be amused. "Taught him a new trick, did you?" She moved to pour herself a cup of coffee.

"He hates eggs," Patrick explained, shoveling another mouthful into Tommy. "So we made a deal—"

"A deal." Thoughtfully, she sipped her coffee. "I see. And exactly what kind of deal was that?" She didn't have the heart to tell him that a two-year-old didn't understand the concept of deals or fair play.

"He gets to spit every other mouthful. The rest he has to eat."

She picked a wad of egg out of Patrick's gleaming black hair. "And how is your...deal working out so far?" she asked, giving Tommy a look that stopped him in his tracks.

His cheeks deflated and he looked crestfallen as he swallowed a mouthful of the dreaded eggs.

Patrick brightened. "Apparently much better since you arrived." He smiled up at her. "How do you feel?"

She dragged a hand through her hair. "Better. Much better. I can actually manage to stand up by myself." She laid a hand on her stomach. "The mischievous druids have stopped dancing in my head, and I think my stomach might be ready to handle some food." She looked at Tommy's eggs with barely disguised disgust. "I'll make my own, thank you."

Laughing, Patrick stood up to hug her, holding her slender body close. "You scared the hell out of me," he whispered against her hair.

She leaned against him, letting him take her weight, allowing him to comfort her. It felt so good to have him there, to know that he'd stayed to look after her, after Tommy.

"I'm sorry." With her arms around his waist, she drew back to look at him. "I didn't mean to." She laid a hand on his cheek. He hadn't shaved in days, and she was quite certain no man had ever looked better. "Thank you, Patrick. I don't know what I would have done without you."

"Brie, there's no need to thank me." He tightened his arms around her. "But I think we need to talk." He glanced at Tommy. "Later."

She nodded, wondering about the look on his face. It caused some concern and made her take a step back, out of his arms, wondering if the past few days had been too much for him. Too much for her to expect. Being Patrick's father certainly didn't include taking care of her and her entire household for several days. She tried to keep the guilt at bay, but it came anyway. "Don't you have to go to work today?"

He shook his head. "It's Saturday. My day off."

Her gaze flew to his and she blinked. "What happened to Friday?"

"You slept through most of it." He turned her toward the window. "See. The snow stopped on Friday. The city is finally digging out and beginning to move. But it's Saturday."

"Saturday," Brie repeated with a shake of her head, feeling numb. It was worse than she'd thought. She'd been nearly incapacitated for over two days.

"Listen, I thought I'd just spend the rest of the weekend here with you and Tommy. Give you a hand until you're on your feet."

Touched beyond measure by his kindness and his words, Brie shook her head. "You've done so much already, Patrick. I'm sure there are other things you need to tend to."

"Nothing as important as you and Tommy." He touched her cheek in that familiar way she'd come to love.

Love.

Oh, Lord, now she'd done it. Staring at him, it struck her hard and fast like a fist to the gut.

She had fallen in love with Patrick Sullivan.

Frightened by the thought, frightened by the feelings that suddenly seemed too big for her to control, Brie took another step backward, wanting—needing—to put some distance between them.

Unaware of the anxiety ripping through her, Patrick smiled. "So go take a shower. I'll finish feeding Tommy, then rustle you up some food."

Too stunned to argue, Brie merely nodded again, wondering what on earth she was going to do.

By Sunday night, Brie felt almost back to normal. True to his word, Patrick had stayed the rest of the weekend, tending to everything. He made food—which was barely edible, so they ended up ordering out—played with Tommy and bathed him, and even saw to Tommy's medicine, disguising the disgusting liquid in any number of things to fool him into taking it.

By the time Patrick put Tommy down for the night, Brie was feeling as physically rested and well as she had in months.

Emotionally was another matter.

She'd been torn asunder by the discovery of her real and deep feelings for Patrick, not certain what to do or how to handle them. Especially now that blood tests proved beyond a shadow of a doubt that he was indeed Tommy's father. During the entire weekend she'd had a hard time remembering that this…coziness, this wonderful togetherness they were enjoying, was not to last. It was only because of circumstances that Patrick was here. She couldn't start imagining the fairy tale, not again. She'd done that once, and had ended up like Humpty Dumpty, falling on her head.

"Tommy's out like a light," Patrick said, padding into the living room in his stocking feet. He'd already lit a fire in the fireplace to ward off the chill of the evening. Although the snow had stopped days ago, an arctic wind had blown in, dragging the temperatures down into single digits.

"Good." Content, she snuggled under the afghan that she kept on the sofa.

"Want to watch a movie?"

Brie shook her head. "No. Actually, I thought we could talk." She patted the seat next to her. "You said the other day we needed to discuss something." She tried to smile, but worry was troubling her heart. "Now that I'm feeling better, this might be a good time."

"All right." Patrick sat down beside her, and took her hand in his.

"Before you begin, Patrick, let me just tell you how much I appreciate all you've done for us this past weekend. With Fiona gone, I don't know what we would have done without you." She looked at him. "I can't ever recall getting sick when Tommy was sick. That was a first, and I'm grateful you were able to be here."

Patrick was looking at their entwined hands, listening. He had to stomp down a flare of anger. He didn't want her gratitude, but something far more. But he didn't know if she was ready to hear it.

He glanced at her, saw the firelight shadowed in her eyes. "Brie, that's what I wanted to talk to you about. I think you know me well enough to know how I feel about Tommy."

She searched his gaze, wondering about the sadness. "Of course."

"He's my son and I love him more than anything in the world."

"I know that, Patrick," she said softly, knowing no truer words were ever spoken. "It's clear how you feel about the boy. It has been from the beginning."

He nodded, grateful she understood. "Then I hope you can understand what I'm about to say." He felt her tense, knew she would have pulled her hand away, so he held on tight. "I don't want to be just a part-time father, Brie. I want to be a full-time, round-the-clock father, just like you're a round-the-clock mother."

She frowned, trying to understand what he was trying to say. A tremor of fear was climbing into her consciousness. "I'm not sure I understand, Patrick. Please, explain yourself."

He nodded. "Brie, what would have happened if I wasn't here this weekend? With Fiona gone—"

"I already told you, Patrick." Her defenses went into high gear, sharpening her voice. "That's never happened before."

"But it happened now, and it could happen again. Fiona won't be here forever. What if you both get sick again? Then what? What would happen to you and Tommy? Who would take care of you?"

That stopped her cold, for she had no easy answer for him, no out because it was a question she couldn't face.

"I'm perfectly capable of taking care of both of us," she said, trying to calm her defenses.

"I know that." He dragged a hand through his hair, knowing what he wanted to say wasn't coming out quite right. He decided to just plunge in with both feet. "Brie, I want you to marry me."

She stared at him in stunned shock for a moment, unable to speak. "I…I…beg your pardon?" She shook her head, dawning horror and dread squeezing her heart. "You want me to marry you because you don't think I'm capable of taking care of your son, is that it? You don't trust me." It hurt far worse than she'd ever thought.

"No, of course not." He sighed, grabbing her hand again, the one she kept slipping out of his. "Brie, listen to me. We agreed that we'd always put Tommy's needs ahead of our own, right?"

She frowned, wondering what this had to do with her marrying him. "Of course—"

"Then you have to see that he deserves two full-time parents. I want the same privileges you have. I want to be here in the middle of the night when he wakes and calls for me. I want to be here to soothe him when he has a nightmare or he's sick."

He wanted to be there for Brie, because whether she knew it or not, whether she admitted it or not, she needed him. As much as he needed her.

"I want to be here the next time Tommy wakes in the middle of the night, sick and feverish. I want all the same rights you have, Brie."

"Rights." It was the only word she'd heard. He wanted...rights. So that was what this was about. His rights. She felt a fierce sense of protectiveness rise up. "I don't understand how marriage to me will give you any further rights to your son." Her voice had gone very soft.

"If we're married, we'll all live together, in the same house. I won't have to leave him after I give him his bath every night. I'll be here in the morning when he wakes up. He'll have two full-time parents, the way it should be."

"I see." She realized now this had nothing to do with marrying her, and everything to do with securing his rights as a parent. "So you've asked me to marry you in order to ensure your parental rights, is that correct?" Something hard and cold had invaded her heart.

"Yes— No!" Patrick dragged a hand through his hair, growing frustrated and furious. This was not going the way he'd intended. "This isn't about securing my rights, Brie. If that was all I was interested in, I would have taken the legal action necessary as my lawyer suggested weeks ago."

She went very cold and very, very still. "Legal action?" She stared at him as if she'd never seen him before. She knew it was a possibility, which was why she'd willingly allowed him into her son's life. To know now that he intended to do it anyway was a crushing blow. "You sought to take legal action against me for Tommy?"

Her words stopped him cold. "No, Brie. I merely found out what my legal rights were."

She never knew it was possible to feel her heart break.

"I see. And did this legal action include marrying me in order to secure your rights as Tommy's father? After all, another woman had betrayed you where your son was concerned. I understand why this might seem logical even…necessary to protect your son."

She didn't understand any of it. Didn't understand that the man she thought she knew wasn't the man standing before her talking of rights and marriage, as if they went together.

Fury stiffened her spine and her shoulders. "Tommy may very well be your son, but he is my son too. As such, I have rights." She forced herself to take a deep breath, to speak slowly and calmly, when all she wanted to do was weep and rage. "I married once, Patrick, and was forced to give up a great deal of my rights—not by choice, mind you, but by law. My husband's law." Her heart, as well. "I vowed then I would never put myself or my son in anyone else's control again."

"Marriage isn't about control, Brie."

Her smile was sad. "Isn't it? Isn't that the whole purpose of your…proposal." She could barely get the word past the lump of tears clogging her throat. "So you can be certain that your rights are protected, that you'll be able to… control me and what happens to your son."

She never thought him capable of treachery and trickery. But she'd been fooled by a man before.

Fooled.

Betrayed.

Disappointed.

And so it was to be again.

She didn't want to hear anymore, couldn't bear to hear anymore. This was what she'd feared most in life. Losing her son. Or losing her heart. She'd foolishly almost done both.

Somehow she had to find her voice. She swallowed hard. "I trusted that you'd keep the agreement we'd made. I've tried to be reasonable and understanding of your needs, to do what's best for Tommy, to put his needs ahead of our own."

"Brie, wait, you don't understand."

"Aye, I understand all too well, Patrick. If you don't make a legal claim to my son, you'll ensure your rights by marrying me."

"No!" He wanted to drag her into his arms, to explain the way he felt. But the look on her face, the tilt of her chin, made him realize she wouldn't listen.

"I won't marry you, Patrick Sullivan." Her chin went up a notch, and her voice trembled with the tears she refused to shed. "I won't put my life or my son's in another man's hands, especially one I can't trust." She speared him with her gaze, and he saw the unshed tears. "And I can see that I can't trust you."

Nothing could have hurt him more. She didn't trust him. It was the worst of his fears. If she didn't trust him, she could never love him. The two went hand in hand. You couldn't have one without the other.

"Brie, that's not true," he protested. "You can trust me."

"Aye, I can see that, Patrick." The smile on her face was far too cold to be one of amusement. "I can trust you to take legal steps to ensure your rights and what's yours. That's what I can trust." She took a deep breath. "And if that fails, then I can trust you to propose a ridiculous marriage in order to ensure those rights. I believed the things you told me, Patrick—that you'd never hurt me or Tommy. But you've lied, haven't you? Is that what I should trust? Your lies?" He tried to interrupt, but she refused to let him. "I don't need you, Patrick." Her voice was deadly calm, but the lie burned her tongue. She needed him more than she'd ever needed anything. But she knew now, it would never be. "I'm perfectly capable of taking care of my son on my own. I've been doing it since his birth, and I'll continue to do it in the future, with or without your help."

She would never make Tommy a pawn between them. She loved the boy far too much for that. But just because Patrick was Tommy's father, and part of the boy's life, didn't mean he had to be part of hers.

She'd see that he wasn't.

"Please go, Patrick." She stood up. If she didn't leave the room, she would collapse in a heap on the floor, weeping.

He reached out to take her shoulders, to stop her. "Brie, wait. Please, listen to me." He wanted to shake her, to throttle her, to force her to listen to him, to explain that she'd taken everything he'd said wrong. But the look on her face, the pain in her eyes, made his guts clench and his tongue twist. He knew no words that could erase such pain.

"Patrick." His name sounded deathly cold on her lips. She looked down at his hands, touching her, remembering a time when she'd welcomed his touch, relished it. Then slowly she lifted her gaze to his. The look in her eyes had him dropping his hands to his sides.

"I've got nothing left to say to you, Patrick. And you've got nothing left to say that I want to hear. I'm sure you know the way out."

She turned away from him, wanting nothing more than to flee into the safety and security of her bedroom. Alone. Where she could deal with her broken heart and her broken dreams in peace.

Patrick was miserable.

It had been two long, lonely days since Brie had banished him from her house. Two days without seeing her or Tommy. She wouldn't take his calls; when he stopped at the shop, she went into her office and shut the door. Unless he wanted to break it down, he had no choice but to accept her cold, calm rejection.

It hurt more than anything he'd ever faced.

He hadn't realized how much a part of his life Brie and Tommy had become. How much he needed them, missed them. He spent the better part of the two days holed up in his apartment, pacing the pattern off the floor.

He realized he'd screwed up big-time. Screwed up because he'd been too afraid to just admit the truth to Brie, because he hadn't realized the truth until it was too late.

He loved her.

Not because she was Tommy's mother. But because of who she was; the woman she was, the person she was. He'd been afraid to admit the truth, afraid to trust another woman, especially where his son was concerned, afraid that once again he would be betrayed.

But it was Brie who felt betrayed.

And he was to blame because he hadn't trusted her or his heart.

How could he have messed up so badly?

Because his fears were all mixed up with his feelings, and until Brie and Tommy had come into his life, nothing had ever been so important to him before.

He'd been so afraid of doing anything to endanger the fragile relationship they had that he'd done the wrong thing. And ruined it.

Now, he simply didn't know how to live with the pain, the loss. Without Brie, without Tommy, there didn't seem to be any purpose in life.

Still pacing the floor of his apartment, Patrick heard the knock at his door. He ignored it. He didn't want to see or talk to anyone. His mother, brothers and even Katie and Joanna had come up to see what was wrong with him. He'd banished them without even opening the door. He wanted to be alone with his pain and his misery. If he had the energy, he would have gotten drunk. But even that didn't appeal to him.

All he knew was that he wanted Brie as his wife, his mate. Even if she hadn't been Tommy's mother, he would have wanted her just the same.

The door burst open. "Patrick, my boy, what's it you're doing up here that's worrying your mother so?" Unmindful of the glare his grandson sent him, Da stepped into the apartment, shutting the door firmly behind him.

"I'm fine, Da."

"Aye, I can see that, lad." Cocking his head, an unlit cigar stuck between two fingers, Da inspected his grandson with wise eyes. "Two days of beard. No food in your stomach for longer than that. You're hiding up here like a wounded bear, growling at the door." Da shook his head. "Fine, indeed." Da rocked back on his heels. "Brie's not much better."

Patrick's head came up. "You've seen Brie?"

"Nay." Da nodded. "Fiona tells me you made the lass cry." Da's voice was grave in a way Patrick hadn't heard since he was ten, and had broken his mother's favorite lamp. "Is that true, son? Have you hurt the lass?"

Guilt-ridden, Patrick nodded his head. "I guess I did." He dragged a hand through his hair. "It wasn't intentional, Da. I wouldn't ever do anything to hurt Brie. Or Tommy," he added, just so there would be no confusion.

"I know that, son," Da said, laying a hand on Patrick's shoulder because the boy looked so miserable. He gave his grandson an affectionate pat. "What is it that you did, boy?"

Patrick's shoulders slumped. "I asked her to marry me."

"I see." Da was thoughtful for a moment. Clearly there was more to this than the boy was telling. He hadn't known any woman to cry, except tears of joy, when a man asked her to be his bride. Nay, he was certain there was something else. "And why did you ask the lass to marry you, boy?"

Patrick waited a moment. "Because I love her, Da." He hadn't realized how true it was, or the depth and breadth of his feelings for Brie until this moment.

"I see." Eyes twinkling, Da tried to bank down a smile. "And did you happen to mention that little fact to her, son?"

Patrick glanced up. "That I loved her?" Miserable, he shook his head. "No."

"Aye." Da nodded his head slowly, then raised his eyes to the heavens. "And the boy wonders why she cries." Eyes twinkling, he shook his head in amusement. "Patrick, if the woman doesn't even know how you feel about her, what makes you think she'd want to throw her lot in with you?"

Glumly Patrick dragged his hands through his hair and paced the length of the living room.

"Da, she completely misunderstood." He glanced at his grandfather, eyes pleading for him to understand. "Brie thinks I asked her to marry me to secure my rights to Tommy. She doesn't know how I feel about her."

"I see." Da smiled, shaking his head, wondering how all three of his grandsons could be such dunderheads, especially about love. But then, he'd not been much smarter. Fortunately, he'd had the love of a good woman, who had shown him the way.

"Patrick, my boy, let me tell you a story." Da paused, choosing his words carefully, twirling his cigar, wishing it were lit. "Before your blessed grandmother died, she told me something I'll never forget."

At the mention of his grandmother, Patrick glanced up. "What, Da?"

"Your lovely grandmother, she held my hand during those last few hours of her life, and she thanked me, son. For loving her, not as the mother of my brood, but for loving her as a woman." There was still awe in Da's voice at the knowledge his beloved Molly had passed to him with her last breaths, knowledge he was eternally grateful for.

Puzzled, Patrick stared at his grandfather. "That's it?"

Da laughed, shaking his head. "Aye. You see, son, we men are so thickheaded at times." Da smiled. "Sometimes we don't put enough emphasis on the things that are important to our women. To the things that matter the most." He paused. "To a woman, once she bears children, she sometimes feels as if the man in her life only sees her as his child's mother, and not as a lovely woman on her own, the woman she was when he fell in love with her. Sometimes, they feel as if our love is just because they're the mother of our children." Da shook his head sadly. "It's a sad fate to do that to a woman, for we only cheat ourselves, lad. We need to show them, to tell them, of our love, not just as mothers, but as our lovers, our women, our partners."

Da grew wistful at the memories. "Your grandmother told me it's a lucky man who remembers to appreciate the woman in his life for being a woman. Even a mother needs to feel special sometimes. And no one can make her feel more special than the man she loves."

Da glanced at his watch. "Brie should be closing the shop about now. I've a mind to have dinner with Fiona. I don't suppose you'd like to give me a lift over?"

Patrick didn't have to be asked twice. He grabbed his

keys and started toward the door, only to have Da lay a hand on his arm.

Grinning, eyes twinkling, Da wrinkled his nose. "Two days it's been, lad, and I think a shave and a wee bit of a shower might be in order first. You don't want to send the lassie running toward her homeland."

Brie was just restocking the shelves with Mrs. Cole's inevitable returns when the bell over the door rang. Forcing a smile she didn't feel, she turned, her eyes going wide. Fiona was supposed to pick Tommy up from his play group, but apparently there had been a change in plans.

"Patrick." Her eyes immediately went to Tommy who was cradled in his father's arms, snowsuit, boots and a fistful of sticky licorice in one hand.

The sight of the two of them together brought tears to her eyes, but she fought them back.

"Ma-ma!" Grinning, Tommy reached out his arm to her, the one holding the licorice. The other was wrapped tightly around his father's neck.

"What are you doing here, Patrick?" Her tone was pleasant, but cold. He looked wonderful, and her heart ached just at the sight of him.

"Tommy and I had some talking to do." He chucked his son under the chin, making the little boy giggle. "Didn't we, son?"

"Talk," Tommy happily mimicked, rolling his head around like a drunken sailor.

She glanced pointedly at her watch. "I've got dinner to make and things to do." She couldn't bear to see him with Tommy, couldn't bear to be with him, knowing what he'd done, what could never be.

"Brie, I'm sorry. I've been a fool. I went about this all wrong."

"I see." One brow rose, and he could see she didn't see, not at all.

"No, you don't. Do you know why I asked you to marry me?"

She nodded, trying to swallow the sudden boulder that seemed lodged in her throat. "To ensure your parental rights to Tommy." She laced her hands together so he wouldn't see them trembling. "Aye, you made the reasons clear enough."

"No, I didn't." He shook his head. "That was part of the problem." He took a deep breath, hoping, praying she'd understand, and give him—them—another chance. "I asked you to marry me, Brie, not to ensure my rights, not because I'm Tommy's father or because you're his mother, but because…I love you." His gaze, pleading, hopeful and filled with love, met hers. "You, Brie, not for any other reason but because I love you. As a woman, a partner, a soul mate."

"Excuse me?" She stared at him, afraid she'd heard wrong.

"I love you, Brie." He lifted a free hand and touched her cheek in the same way he'd done so many times before.

Tommy immediately mimicked him, laying his sticky licorice hand on Brie's other cheek, his curious glance going from his stunned mother to his hopeful father.

"I—let me explain. Please?" Patrick waited for her nod to continue. "I know how important it is for you to know that you can take care of yourself and Tommy, for you not to need anyone, especially a man. And I know how hard it is for you to trust someone, especially where Tommy is concerned." His gaze sought hers. "I thought I'd shown you that I'd never do anything to hurt either of you." His voice grew soft. "I didn't know if you'd ever be able to trust me or need me, and so I thought…I thought…if we were married, that maybe eventually, you'd come to love me, and then maybe even need and trust me…" His voice trailed off. "I guess I sort of did this backward. I love you, Brie, and what I feel for you has nothing to do with Tommy or the fact that you're his mother. I love you because you're you. I want you to marry me, and make a home with me—for us—and for our son. Because you want to, and because you love me, not for any other reason."

"Oh, Patrick." Her vision blurred and her throat clogged. She'd been too afraid to hope, too afraid to dream, for herself and her son, until Patrick Sullivan walked into her life and made all her hopes and dreams come true.

She stared at him, her heart full of hope, full of love. She had a choice to make. She could take a risk, and give him another chance. Or she could remain afraid to trust, afraid to love, afraid to live.

She could listen to her heart. Or listen to her mind.

For her, there was no choice.

"I love you, too, Patrick." She leaned up and brushed her lips against his, letting out a relieved sigh she felt she'd been holding forever.

His arms went around her, and he dragged her close, with Tommy squashed between them. Brie let the tears come, but this time they were tears of joy, of love, of happiness.

She'd been given a second chance at love, and she'd be a fool not to take it.

"And I do need you, Patrick. Like I've never needed or wanted anyone else," she whispered, laying a gentle hand to his cheek. "Aye, as much as the air I breathe." Her eyes slid closed, and she leaned against him, letting the feelings, the emotions swamp her. She felt gloriously lucky and alive. "And yes, Patrick, I will marry you."

She'd marry him, and love him, and raise his child, and

grow old with him. All the things—the only things—she'd ever wanted.

Patrick pressed his lips to her temple. "I need you, too, Brie. Always." He kissed her again, as the tears slipped down her cheeks. "Not just as Tommy's mother, but as my wife."

"Ma-ma cry?" Tommy nudged his sticky face between them, patting his mother's cheeks in comfort. "Cry, Mama?" Tilting his head back and forth, he studied her with somber eyes.

Laughing, she hugged him, wiping her tears as Patrick planted kisses across her temple. "No, Mama's not crying."

"Kiss!" Tommy lifted his face toward his father, wanting to get into the act. "Da kiss!"

Patrick happily obliged, planting a loud, smacking kiss on his son's sticky, chubby cheek, fulfilled in a way that brought such joy to his heart he thought it would fly right out of his chest.

Brie watched them, the two men in her life, the two men she loved more than anything in the world. She was absolutely certain there wasn't a luckier woman alive.

"Dogs?" Tommy asked hopefully, pressing his face against Patrick's and playing patty-cake on his father's cheeks. "Dogs, Da?"

"Uh-oh," Patrick muttered under his breath, making Brie lift a brow.

She laughed at the twin looks of mischief on their faces. "I don't suppose he's making his dinner choice known, is he?"

"Tattletale," Patrick whispered, making Tommy giggle. "We were going to break this to her gently, son."

"Break what to me gently, Patrick?" she asked, trying not to grin.

Tommy kicked his feet, pushing away to slither down the length of his father, holding on to Patrick's long legs for balance. Once he was secure on his own booted feet, he took off through the shop toward the door, dropping licorice candy in his wake.

"Dog!" he squealed, bouncing up and down and pointing out the window.

"Oh, my Lord," Brie muttered, as she followed on Patrick's heels, wanting to see what her son was pointing to. "It is a...dog," she nearly squeaked.

The animal was peering out the window of Patrick's car, looking woeful and sad. The moment she saw Tommy, she started jumping and barking. The dog was big enough, the sound loud enough to rumble the sidewalk.

Obviously delighted, Tommy grabbed Brie's leg and hung on. "Dog, Ma-ma."

"Yes, I can see that, love." She laid a hand on Tommy's head to balance him, but her gaze went to Patrick's. He grinned the grin that made her heart turn over. Brie chewed her lip, then looked at the sad, forlorn thing out in the cold. "I thought you said it was a...puppy?"

"It is," Patrick confirmed, scooping Tommy up in his arms once again so the boy could get a better look. Tommy leaned out of his father's arms to press his nose to the frosty glass, waving frantically at his new pet.

"It looks more like a horse," Brie commented sourly, trying to work up annoyance and not quite managing it.

"She's just a baby, Brie." Patrick dropped his free arm around her shoulder and dragged her close. "Wait until she grows."

"Grows?" she whispered in horror, still staring at the animal that took up Patrick's entire front seat. "Patrick, what on earth am I supposed to do with her?"

He turned to her, his eyes shining with love. "What you

do best, Brie." He leaned forward and captured her lips with his. "Love her." He kissed her again until her knees were weak and her head was spinning.

She nodded dully. "I can do that." She frowned, not quite clear exactly what it was she thought she could do. "I suppose."

Laughing, Patrick dragged her close. He kissed her again, his arms wrapped securely around his son and the woman he loved. "I love you, Brie."

"Aye, and I love you, too, Patrick." She rested her head on his chest, allowing herself to lean on him, knowing she'd finally found a warm, safe—permanent—place to rest her weary head."

"Da?" With a sticky hand, Tommy turned Patrick's face to his. "Da?"

Patrick grinned, bouncing his son in his arms. "What, son?"

"Cat, Da?" Tommy grinned. "Cat? Pease?"

"Cat?" Brie drew back in horror. "Patrick, you have to stop teaching him these new words." She shook her head firmly. "No cat, Tommy." She glanced at Patrick, and saw his grin. "Absolutely, positively no cats, Patrick Sullivan."

"Michael's triplets just got a cute little calico. Wait until Tommy sees him."

"No." She shook her head. "Absolutely not."

Tommy leaned in and gave her a wet sloppy kiss. "Pease, Ma-ma. Cat?"

She moaned, wondering what she was going to do with these men in her life. What she was meant to do all along, she thought as she looked at them. Love them.

"Pease?"

"All right." She sighed. "Maybe one cat. A little one. I'll think about it." Knowing Patrick, he'd probably come home with a mountain lion.

Grinning, Patrick guided his family through the store. "How do you feel about horses, Brie? I thought it might be something good for Tommy—"

"No, no, no. Absolutely not."

"Maybe a parakeet, then."

"Patrick, where are we going?" she asked abruptly, realizing he was hustling her toward the back door and distracting her the whole while.

"To meet my family." He glanced at her. "We have to tell them there's going to be another wedding in the family." He paused and looked at her for a long moment. "Are you sure, Brie?" He had to know she was sure, that there were no doubts, no fears. "Are you sure you're ready?"

"Ready?" She grinned, slipping her arm around him. "Patrick, love, I've been ready for you my whole life."

Epilogue

Their wedding was a true Sullivan family affair. On the eve of the New Year, with the pub filled to the rafters with various Sullivan cousins, nieces, nephews, aunts and uncles, Brie and Patrick, with their son Tommy between them, recited their vows. Katie and Joanna Sullivan stood up for Brie, while Michael and Danny Sullivan stood up for their baby brother, Patrick.

Dressed in a simple ivory suit with matching shoes, Brie stood beside Patrick, in front of their families, their friends and their son, pledging their life and their love.

The moment the ceremony was over the rousing celebration began.

"It's a fine, fine day for a wedding." Puffing on a large, smelly cigar, Da bent and kissed Brie's cheek, his eyes shining with pride. "Now you're a tried-and-true Sullivan. As is your boy." Da nodded. "As it should be."

Carefully he draped an arm around her shoulders, puffing vigorously on his cigar, blowing a heavy stream of smoke in the air, hoping Fiona wouldn't catch him. A man should be able to enjoy a good cigar on the day of his youngest grandson's wedding.

Glancing around at the assembled guests, Da nodded. "You've made me a proud man today, lass, a proud man indeed." He glanced across the room to where Fiona was holding Tommy. His smiled broadened every time he looked at his great-grandson. And the woman holding him. "Aye, and a happy one, as well." Grinning, he puffed out his chest in pride. "You've given me another grandson. And a black-haired blue-eyed Irishman at that." Da chuckled. "How lucky can one man be?"

"Da." Brie leaned up on tiptoe to kiss him. "I'm the lucky one. You—all of you—have been wonderful to me and Tommy. Making us feel welcome, bringing us into the fold of the family."

Her fears had been for naught. The Sullivans, from the youngest to the oldest, had welcomed her and her child into their family as if they'd always belonged. She'd instantly fallen in love with all of them, especially Da. He reminded her so much of her own father, gone all these long years now.

"My father would have been proud to know you, Da," she whispered, kissing his cheek again. "Proud, indeed."

He drew back, truly perplexed. "Of course he would have, lassie. How could he not?" Laughing, Brie hugged him tight.

"Ma-ma!" Dodging guests, Tommy barreled toward her with Fiona fast on his heels. His hair was mussed, his little tuxedo was askew, and somehow his bow tie was hanging at half-mast. There was something dark and sticky around his mouth. It looked suspiciously like…licorice.

"Come here, you little imp." Handing Brie his cigar, Da bent down to scoop the boy up in his arms, juggling him expertly. "Running from Grandma Grouch again?" Da glanced at Fiona who had stopped to catch her breath. "Is that it, boy?" Da nuzzled Tommy's cheek, enjoying the baby-sweet smell of him.

"Da!" Clapping his hands against Da's cheeks, Tommy's eyes gleamed with mischief. "Candy?" Tommy pressed his nose to Da's. "Candy, pease?" he begged, eyes pleading.

Laughing, Da glanced around, surprised to find Brie watching him as he reached into his pocket to extract one of the little black candies the little imp liked so much.

"You're spoiling him," Brie said, trying not to grin.

"Aye, of course." Da grinned. "What else am I to do with the boy?"

"Honey?" Patrick came up next to Brie, sliding his arm around her. He couldn't resist, he pressed a kiss to her lips. "It's time to go. The limo is here."

"Go?" She looked at Patrick, then at the baby. She'd never left Tommy before. A trickle of fear raced over her. "Now?"

Patrick laughed. "Sweetheart, we're only going to be gone a week. It's our honeymoon." He glanced at Tommy, and ruffled his hair. "He'll be fine. Da, Fiona and everyone else in the family plans to take care of him. He won't even notice we're gone." Patrick drew back and looked at her. "Would you rather not go?"

"No!" The chance to be alone with Patrick for a whole blissful week with no responsibilities, no timetable, nothing but Patrick and love was too tempting to even consider giving up.

"So you've got the little one again," Fiona said, huffing up to them. She spotted the lit cigar in Brie's hand and snatched it free. "Be off with you now," she ordered, holding the cigar out of Da's reach. She leaned over and kissed Brie, then motioned Patrick down so she could kiss him, as well. "Enjoy yourselves," she said with a tear and a smile. She glanced at Da and Tommy. "And don't worry, I'll see to them, and the shop."

Brie gave her a quick, hard hug. "Thank you for everything, Fiona. I love you."

"Aye, child, and I love you."

As Brie and Patrick slipped away, Fiona turned to Da with a scowl. "Smelling up the day with this stinky stick?" She held his cigar aloft for a moment, and Da's heart sunk. He could kiss his last cigar goodbye now for sure. "Enough is enough, Sean Sullivan." He watched in dismay as Fiona marched to a pitcher of water sitting on a table and dunked his cigar in it.

"Ouch, boy," he said to Tommy. "Your grandma's done it again."

"Ouch," Tommy mimicked, making a fist to rub his tired eyes.

"The lad's a bit sleepy," Da said to Fiona.

"He's missed his nap." She glanced around at the crowd. "Too many people, too much food and too much excitement." She turned to Da with a glare that was ruined by the smile sneaking around the corners of her mouth. "Not to mention all the licorice you've been stuffing into him."

"Aye, lass, you wound me. Wound me, I say." Eyes twinkling, he reached for her hand. "Let's put the imp down for a bit." Taking her hand, he led her to a quiet part of the pub, where the Sullivan family cradle was resting. Da plopped Tommy right smack down in the middle, watching as the boy giggled as it began to sway to and fro.

Fiona ran her hand along the fine, intricately carved wood. "It's a beauty," she commented softly. "I've not seen anything like it since I left Ireland."

Pleased, Da pulled out two chairs, and motioned her to

sit. "I suppose, lassie, it's time to teach the boy about his clan." He looked at Fiona pointedly. "The *Sullivan* clan," he specified, lest there be any mistake.

"Ah, there were six of us, and we were a wild and handsome bunch." Laughing, Da glanced at the cradle, the memories of his youth flooding him. "A long time ago, lass, well, one of the Sullivan brothers—and a handsome fellow at that—fell madly in love with a fine and beautiful lass." Eyes shining, Da glanced at the little imp, snuggling down into the cradle. Tommy's eyes were drooping as if someone had dropped a pebble on them. "Well, this pretty little lass was named Molly and her hair was red, and her smile charming." Da sighed heavily, wishing for his cigar. "But alas, Molly was pledged to another." He grinned suddenly, remembering the mischief and mayhem that had ensued. "But like I said, we were the Sullivan brothers and not known for accepting defeat. So one of the brothers, the one in love with Molly, cooked up a plan, and a fine grand plan it was. He couldn't bear the thought of his love pledged to another, nor could he accept living his life without her. So on the night before her match, when all was quiet, he and his brothers snuck into her camp and stole her."

"Stole her?" Fiona asked, not certain if she should be horrified or amused.

"As the saints are above," Da said in confirmation. "On that night, his own brothers helped him spirit his love away from their homeland and onto a fishing boat that would begin a journey that would take them to their new homeland. America." Da's eyes misted as he thought of that time long ago, and all that had happened since. "It was a journey of new beginnings. All they had to their names was this cradle, the one the little imp is now sleeping in." Da reached down and stroked Tommy's hair, his eyes shining with love. "Ah, lass, this cradle was her wedding present, something to show his eternal love, something to pass on to future generations so they would always know of that love." His voice grew soft as he looked at Fiona. "They had a wonderful, happy life together, full of mischief and an abundance of love, until the day his Molly girl drew her last breath."

"Sean." Fiona reached for him, took his hand, held it to her heart. "Aye, you loved her so."

He nodded. "I did, there's no denying it."

"I'm sorry."

He laughed, kissing her hand. "For what? We had a beautiful life and a wonderful family." He glanced around the room, his gaze drifting to his beloved family. "This is our legacy. What we always wanted." His gaze traveled to his grandsons.

Mikey. So strong, so proud and now with a beautiful wife, a beautiful daughter and three healthy strapping sons.

Danny. So stubborn and headstrong, and so very much like him, he thought with a laugh. He'd found his love in Katie, and now they had their own little girl, Molly, and another on the way.

And finally Patrick. The youngest. Patrick had finally found happiness with a beautiful lass who had given him the greatest gift of all: a son.

There was a whole new generation of Sullivans to carry on the legacy he and Molly had started. She might be gone, but the evidence of her life, their love, was everywhere around him.

Da glanced down at Tommy. He was curled into a ball. His little tuxedo pants were hiked up to his chubby little calfs. One shoe was lost, his thumb was stuck in his mouth, and he was snoring like a steam engine.

Overwhelmed with love, Da touched the boy, letting the love from one generation flow to another.

Aye, it had been a long, wonderful journey since that night he had stood on the cliffs, letting the rain take his tears, cursing the fates for taking his love. He'd been a young man then, filled with a young man's dreams and a young man's love.

He was no longer young.

He glanced at Fiona. To his surprise, he found he could still love. A new love, a different kind of love, the kind that filled the empty spot his Molly had left. Not to replace, but to add to his life.

He reached out and stroked the cradle, knowing Molly would have approved. After all these years, he'd finally stopped grieving. The ache in his heart had been replaced with something new, something warm, something he'd almost forgotten existed.

He kissed Fiona's hand again.

Clearing his throat, he chose his words carefully. He might not be a young man any longer, but he still had a young man's butterflies about something as important as this.

"Now that Brie is going to be moving in with Patrick, that apartment of yours is going to be very empty."

"Aye." Fiona sighed slowly, nodding her head in agreement. "Empty indeed."

"Perhaps you might consider sharing it?"

Her eyes twinkled. "Are you asking me to live in sin, Sean Sullivan?"

"No, lass." His eyes so blue, so steady, stayed on hers. "I'm asking you, lass, to live with me…in love." He held her hand, his heart in his mouth.

"Oh, Sean." Fiona's eyes closed so he wouldn't see the tears of joy. "Aye, I guess I have no choice. If I left you alone, you'd be smoking those stinking sticks, wouldn't you?"

"Indeed." Pleased, he nodded. "So is that a yes, Fiona McGee?"

"It is."

He lifted her hand and kissed it again. The cradle which had stopped, suddenly, slowly, started rocking again. Da watched it for a moment, feeling a lightness in his heart. He glanced up at the heavens and smiled.

"Thank you, Molly girl," he whispered. "I knew you'd approve."

* * * * *

Catch more great

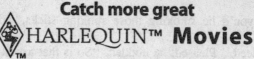

HARLEQUIN™ **Movies**

featured on the movie channel tmc

Premiering August 8th
The Waiting Game
Based on the novel by *New York Times*
bestselling author Jayne Ann Krentz

Don't miss next month's movie!
Premiering September 12th
A Change of Place
Starring Rick Springfield and
Stephanie Beacham. Based on the novel
by bestselling author Tracy Sinclair

If you are not currently a subscriber to
The Movie Channel, simply call your
local cable or satellite provider for more
details. Call today, and don't miss out
on the romance!

the movie channel tmc

100% pure movies.
100% pure fun.

HARLEQUIN®

Makes any time special ™

Take 2 bestselling love stories FREE

Plus get a FREE surprise gift!

Special Limited-Time Offer

Mail to Silhouette Reader Service™

> 3010 Walden Avenue
> P.O. Box 1867
> Buffalo, N.Y. 14240-1867

YES! Please send me 2 free Silhouette Romance™ novels and my free surprise gift. Then send me 6 brand-new novels every month, which I will receive months before they appear in bookstores. Bill me at the low price of $2.90 each plus 25¢ delivery and applicable sales tax, if any.* That's the complete price, and a saving of over 10% off the cover prices—quite a bargain! I understand that accepting the books and gift places me under no obligation ever to buy any books. I can always return a shipment and cancel at any time. Even if I never buy another book from Silhouette, the 2 free books and the surprise gift are mine to keep forever.

215 SEN CH7S

Name	(PLEASE PRINT)	
Address	Apt. No.	
City	State	Zip

This offer is limited to one order per household and not valid to present Silhouette Romance™ subscribers. *Terms and prices are subject to change without notice. Sales tax applicable in N.Y.

USROM-98   ©1990 Harlequin Enterprises Limited

HE CAN CHANGE A DIAPER IN THREE SECONDS FLAT
BUT CHANGING HIS MIND ABOUT MARRIAGE MIGHT
TAKE SOME DOING! HE'S ONE OF OUR

Fabulous Fathers

July 1998

ONE MAN'S PROMISE by Diana Whitney (SR#1307)

He promised to be the best dad possible for his daughter. Yet when successful architect Richard Matthews meets C. J. Moray, he wants to make another promise—this time to a wife.

September 1998

THE COWBOY, THE BABY AND THE BRIDE-TO-BE
by Cara Colter (SR#1319)

Trouble, thought Turner MacLeod when Shayla Morrison showed up at his ranch with his baby nephew in her arms. Could he take the chance of trusting his heart with this shy beauty?

November 1998

ARE YOU MY DADDY? by Leanna Wilson (SR#1331)

She hated cowboys, but Marty Thomas was willing to do anything to help her son get his memory back—even pretend sexy cowboy Joe Rawlins was his father. Problem was, Joe thought he might like this to be a permanent position.

Available at your favorite retail outlet, only from

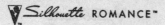

Silhouette ROMANCE™

Look us up on-line at: http://www.romance.net

SRFFJ-N

SILHOUETTE® *Desire*®

THE RULE BREAKERS

an exciting new series by
Leanne Banks

Meet The Rulebreakers: A millionaire, a bad boy, a protector. Three strong, sexy men who take on the ultimate challenge—love!

Coming in September 1998—MILLIONAIRE DAD

Joe Caruthers had it all. Who would have thought that a brainy beauty like Marley Fuller—pregnant with his child—would cause this bachelor with everything to take the plunge?

Coming in October 1998—
THE LONE RIDER TAKES A BRIDE

Bad boy Ben Palmer had rebelled against falling in love, until he took the lovely, sad-eyed Amelia Russell on a moonlit ride.

Coming in November 1998—THIRTY-DAY FIANCÉ

Nick Nolan had to pretend to be engaged to his childhood friend Olivia Polnecek. Why was Nick noticing how perfect a wife she could be—for real!

Available at your favorite retail outlet.

Silhouette®

Look us up on-line at: http://www.romance.net

SDRULE

COMING NEXT MONTH

#1318 THE GUARDIAN'S BRIDE—Laurie Paige
Virgin Brides

She was beautiful, intelligent—and too young for him! But Colter McKinnon was committed to making sure Belle Glamorgan got properly married. Still, how was he supposed to find her an appropriate husband when all Colter really wanted was to make her *his* bride?

#1319 THE COWBOY, THE BABY AND THE BRIDE-TO-BE—Cara Colter
Fabulous Fathers

Handing over a bouncing baby boy to Turner MacLeod at his Montana ranch was just the adventure Shayla Morrison needed. But once she got a look at the sexy cowboy-turned-temporary-dad, she hoped her next adventure would be marching down the aisle with him!

#1320 WEALTH, POWER AND A PROPER WIFE
Karen Rose Smith
Do You Take This Stranger?

Being the proper wife of rich and powerful Christopher Langston was *almost* the fairy tale she had once dreamed of living. But sweet Jenny was hiding a secret from her wealthy husband—and once revealed, the truth could bring them even closer together…or tear them apart forever.

#1321 HER BEST MAN—Christine Scott
Men!

What was happening to her? One minute Alex Trent was Lindsey Richards's best friend, and the next moment he'd turned into the world's sexiest hunk! Alex now wanted to be more than friends—but could he convince Lindsey to trust the love he wanted to give.

#1322 HONEY OF A HUSBAND—Laura Anthony

Her only love was back in town, and he had Daisy Hightower trembling in her boots. For, if rugged loner Kael Carmody ever learned that her son was also his, there would be a high price to pay…maybe even the price of marriage.

#1323 TRUE LOVE RANCH—Elizabeth Harbison

The last thing Darcy Beckett wanted was to share her inherited ranch with ex-love Joe Tyler for two months. But when Joe and his young son showed up, the sparks started flying. Now Joe's son wants the two months to go on forever…and so does Joe! Can he convince Darcy they are the family she's always wanted?